Legends
of
Akelian

Legends of Akelian

TALES FROM THE ELVISH REALMS

MJ FOULKS

iUniverse

Legends of Akelian
Tales from the Elvish Realms

iUniverse books may be ordered through booksellers or by contacting:

iUniverse
1663 Liberty Drive
Bloomington, IN 47403
www.iuniverse.com
1-800-Authors (1-800-288-4677)

Because of the dynamic nature of the Internet, any web addresses or links contained in this book may have changed since publication and may no longer be valid. The views expressed in this work are solely those of the author and do not necessarily reflect the views of the publisher, and the publisher hereby disclaims any responsibility for them.

Any people depicted in stock imagery provided by Thinkstock are models, and such images are being used for illustrative purposes only. Certain stock imagery © Thinkstock.

ISBN: 978-1-4917-6001-7 (sc)
ISBN: 978-1-4917-6002-4 (e)

Library of Congress Control Number: 2015901924

Print information available on the last page.

iUniverse rev. date: 03/09/2015

For Alexis,
may you be the first
to ever venture
to the world of Akelian.

Contents

The River and the Race

Normal human boys spent all of their time with their friends, hanging out on the stone streets in front of their houses--and when normal human boys wanted to race, they sprinted down their stone streets. But in these ancient days of the Earth, this was no gray street, and Demetri was no normal boy.

The wind blew through his sandy hair as he dashed along a muddy river bank in the middle of a deep forest, expertly dancing around the trees, barefooted, as the crunching sound of rapidly approaching footsteps echoed behind him.

"Give it up Darion!" Demetri shouted back to his twin brother straggling behind. "You'll never catch up to me now!"

"That's....what you think..." Darion huffed from behind him, gasping for breath. "I have...an advantage!"

"Hah! No you--arrgh!!" Demetri shouted as he felt a sharp stab in the bottom his bare foot. His knees buckled and he fell, face first, into the muddy river bank. After rolling over and wincing slightly, he found a thorned branch embedded into his heel.

Darion skipped up from behind him, not even out of breath anymore, with a wide smirk on his face.

"I have *shoes*," he laughed mockingly.

Demetri growled and stuck out his tongue at his brother. Just like with most twins, Demetri and Darion looked very much alike, but were not perfect copies of one another. They both had the same sandy blond hair and the same three freckles on their right cheeks in the shape of perfect triangles. Demetri was just the slightest bit thinner and more muscular (he greatly enjoyed climbing trees), and Darion was slightly more plump (he greatly enjoyed berry pie). Where Demetri had eyes of vivid green, Darion's eyes were tranquil blue. In the end, if the two of them could somehow keep their eyes hidden, they would look nearly exactly alike.

Demetri stared at the branch, sulking. Five thorns were stuck in his heel, and beads of blood were forming around them. He pulled gently on the branch, but it wouldn't budge.

Out of nowhere, a bright red fox dashed right up to him and began licking the mud off of his face.

"Ugh! Ew, yuck!" Demetri sputtered. "Thanks, Amphy. Real big help you are."

"Don't take your stupidity out on your pet," Darion said as he reached down and stroked Amphy on the head.

"He's *your* pet, not mine," Demetri scoffed, gently pulling on the thorny branch once again.

"Let me try," Darion said as he quickly leaned over Demetri's foot.

"No, Dare, I can do it! No!"

With striking speed, Darion grabbed the branch and yanked on it.

"OWW! DARE, WHAT IS WRONG WITH YOU?!" Demetri shouted with pain, but looked up to see Darion standing there with the bloody branch in his hand, a glint of victory in his brilliant blue eyes.

"Better to do it quickly than a little bit at a time. Mom told me that," he said coolly as he sat down in the mud right beside his brother.

Demetri just rolled his green eyes. "Thanks, I guess."

Amphy knelt down and started licking Demetri's wound, making him cringe. "Can you tell your fox to stop licking me?"

"He's your fox too," said Darion again impatiently. "He's just trying to help, and with how many times you hurt yourself, you need all the help you can get."

"Har har har, Dare," Demetri snickered as he scratched behind Amphy's ear absentmindedly, staring out to the river in the distance. Darion tore the sleeve off of his shirt and carefully wrapped it around

Demetri's foot, which was now bleeding freely. "Just for the walk home," he said, leaning back on his elbows.

"Thanks," Demetri muttered, trying not to think about how painful the hike home would be.

The muddy earth slowly seeped through his clothes as he rested there, sure that Darion was getting thoroughly filthy as well. He continued to stare in silence at the rushing river, glimmering in the sunlight. The sun's rays danced merrily through the leaves high above them, landing on their cheeks as they sat there in content silence.

Akelian was the enchanting land that the boys called home, living in a remote forest somewhere in the middle of this vast, magical land. It was filled with more wonder than the boys could ever explore, but Demetri was determined to see every single inch of it in his lifetime. As an eleven year old boy in the middle of the woods, he was itching to go out and find adventure, hopefully dragging his twin brother along with him.

But at the end of the day, the itch just couldn't be helped. With his mother, father, and Grandmother telling glorious stories about the land and the spectacular times they had out there, Demetri couldn't stop himself from brimming with curiosity. He and Darion had spent most of their lives under the shelter of the forest... there was so much he had never seen...so much he didn't know...

What he did know what that Akelian had six kingdoms, each with its own special majesty...but only one kingdom belonged to the humans...and they were far from alone in this world...

The human kingdom lay somewhere in the distant east, right on the ocean, the so-called glorious kingdom of Bellumor... and the boys knew all about it. Once upon a time, they lived in a gray stone house on a gray stone street, not a single tree to be found anywhere. Demetri always thought of Bellumor's treeless lands as incredibly depressing, sucking all of the imagination out of life. Everything in that kingdom was stone and earth, and very boring.

On one particularly boring day, their Dad came home with a smile on his face, but coldness in his voice. He told everyone to gather up all of their belongings as quickly as they could, saying it was time to move on. He didn't tell them why they needed to leave, only that they were off to better things.

Demetri could remember the family walking briskly through the stone kingdom doors as he jumped up and down, a mere boy of four years old, unable to contain his excitement and ready for his first great adventure. Darion, on the other hand, had a very sullen face and sad walk. A pendant of brown stone hung around his neck with the symbol of Bellumor etched carefully into it, and he kept his little fist wrapped around it as the kingdom doors faded into the distance behind them. With Demetri skipping and Darion sulking, the boys held hands as they turned away from the kingdom of their birth, never to return.

His family finally settled down close to the river that had become their favorite racing path. He was unsure exactly why his

Dad had chosen this forest, but according to him, there was no place safer for their family. The crystal clear river cut through the deep, emerald forests just north of one very special kingdom, Rhodarion.

Demetri's father told him stories about the beauty of this wonderful kingdom. It had beautiful forests and massive snow covered mountains, but as beautiful and magical as the land was, it was nothing compared to its inhabitants.

The kingdom of Rhodarion belonged to a very special race of creatures called elves, and Demetri was obsessed with them. These creatures were much smaller than humans, only ever reaching about four and a half feet tall, but they were strikingly beautiful. According to the twins' father, elves in Rhodarion had soft, raven hair and rich brown eyes, with silky smooth skin and long ears, with youthful, innocent faces that glowed with natural beauty.

But as beautiful as these creatures were, it wasn't just their good looks that kept Demetri's fascination...It was their enchanting powers.

Rhodarion was home to elves that could wield fire with their bare hands.

His father once told him that they could command fire to do whatever they wanted it to do. They could even scoop it up and shoot it hundreds of feet away, setting whatever they wanted ablaze. Demetri smiled, imagining how cool it would be to hold fire in his hand without getting burned...

"You know, you may be faster than me, but you'll never beat me until you start wearing shoes," said Darion, jarring Demetri from his thoughts.

"Shoes do nothing," Demetri retorted, "but numb the bottom of your feet. I have the advantage because I can feel the earth and leaves under my feet as I run, just like the elves can."

"And the sharp rocks, thorns, and bees..." Darion muttered under his breath.

"I only stepped on a bee once!" Demetri said defensively.

A smile formed in the corner of Darion's mouth as he stood up, brushing the damp soil from his behind. "Besides, Dad said the elves wear shoes too," he reminded him, holding his hand out to help Demetri to his feet. "They got them from the humans."

Demetri grunted. "That's not true! Humans got their shoes from the elves!"

"So the elves do wear shoes, eh?" Darion smirked.

"Okay, so they do wear shoes," Demetri conceded with a mumble. "But they didn't get them from humans! The elves came first and the humans took the idea from them."

Darion rolled his eyes, giving a sarcastic chuckle as they started their trek back through the thick woods, with Demetri leaning on Darion's shoulder. Amphy trotted slowly behind, sniffing the ground as he went along.

It was no secret that Darion didn't share his brother's love of the magical elves, but he didn't just lack fascination in them--he resented them. *That's probably why he refuses to give them credit for their own inventions and breakthroughs*, Demetri thought to himself as they limped further down the muddy trail.

Their father never did explain to them why they had to leave the kingdom, not even

as they got older...but Darion had come to
his own conclusions. Unlike Demetri, Darion
had a great many little friends while they
lived in Bellumor. All of his friends' parents
hated the elves, so his friends did as well...
but when he went home, he heard nothing
but praises for elves from his family. Darion
had always assumed that their parents had
to leave because their elf-loving ways drove
them out of an elf-hating world. If it weren't
for the elves, their parents wouldn't have
been shunned by the rest of the kingdom,
and they wouldn't have been forced to leave.
So, from the day that they left, Darion
harbored a deep resentment toward the
elves--one that he carried alone--

The boys hobbled slowly through the
dense forest, Amphy trotting just behind
them. After nearly an hour's worth of painful
limping and shuffling, they finally came
upon the sunny clearing with the small
wooden cottage that had been their home for
the past seven years. Amphy looked up at
the boys and then trotted happily toward the
cottage ahead of them.

A frail old woman was sitting in her rocking chair, a green blanket draped over her lap. Her gray hair was so long that it fell in piles onto the floor, piles that were nearly flattened by the chair runners as she peacefully rocked back and forth. Darion's mouth widened into a smirk at the sight of her.

"Shall we settle this once and for all?" he asked as if he were trying to make a bet.

"Settle what?" Demetri breathed heavily, not caring about much more than dinner and a fresh bandage.

"Gema's awake. Let's go say hi. Then she can tell you that humans came before the elves," Darion said teasingly, but Demetri just rolled his eyes.

"You know that's not true, so you're just setting yourself up for disappointment."

They slowly limped and lumbered up to their sunlit front porch, where Gema's round and worn face smiled warmly at them. She brushed some stray strands of hair out of her face, looking down at Demetri's foot.

"You hurt yourself again, Tree?" she said with a chuckle.

"Only a little bit," he lied, blushing. "My feet are getting really tough so it doesn't even hurt."

"Your mother is not going to be happy about you wandering in the woods without shoes again, young man," Gema said in a stern voice, but winked at him with a mischievous smile. Demetri smiled back, and he and Darion both took a seat on their identical stools right in front of Gema's rocker.

"Amphy," Gema called out in a singsong voice as she pulled a thin scrap of dried meat from under her blanket. Amphy jumped up onto his hind legs, panting and wagging his pleading tail. Gema smiled and let out a small giggle.

"Come on, dance for me," she chimed. Amphy jumped on his hind legs in a circle.

"Haha, good boy!" she said, beaming as she threw the meat high into the air--Amphy caught it in his mouth, his tail wagging wildly.

"Gema, will you please tell Tree that the humans were the first beings in Akelian?" Darion blurted out quickly. "He keeps trying to say that the elves were here before humans."

Gema let out a soft giggle. "My dear Dare, I can't tell you that, because it isn't true."

"HA! HAHAHAHA!! I told you!" Demetri hopped up and down on his uninjured foot. "The elves came first! The elves came first!" he sang tauntingly.

"I didn't say that, Tree," Gema interrupted. Feeling deflated, Demetri stopped dancing.

"But--"

"Your brother asked me if humans were the first beings on earth, and that is not true."

"So it was the elves--"

"No, grandson," she interrupted. "It was neither of them."

The twins stared at her, both confused. She simply stared back at them with a mischievous grin before gingerly standing, her long hair hovering only inches from the floor.

"Stay here," she whispered, and shuffled through the front door of the cottage.

such a thing had never been heard of, and
it had to be impossible. The great endless
ocean...coming to an end?

Slowly and carefully, he swam toward
this strange phenomenon, keeping as much
of his body in the water as possible. Closer
and closer he swam, yet the mass remained
perfectly still. His belly brushed onto the
bottom of the ocean floor, and he was as
close to the exposed surface as he could get;
the water's surface rested just below his
eyes.

The waves broke endlessly on this stretch
of dry emptiness, but didn't crash over the
emptiness itself. He looked as far into the
distance as he could, trying to find an end
to this strange thing. The brilliant blue
sky met with the emptiness in the distant
horizon--it could have gone on forever. No
seaweed, clams, or even plankton could be
found anywhere in this eerie, empty mass
of nothing. *How could this be possible?*
he thought to himself, feeling a sickness
swelling his stomach.

He gazed at the eternal nothing, longing
to help, but lost without ideas. He thought

and he thought, racking his brain without taking his eyes off of the strange nothing. Suddenly, he felt the currents in his mind all come together, and an idea struck him. If he could push it beneath the surface of the ocean, the life giving waters would heal the nothingness. Fish would come to live here, coral, crabs, and even dolphins.

He thought some more.

Even as large and powerful as he was, he knew he did not have the power to raise the ocean high enough to submerge the nothingness...

There was nothing for it. He had to sink the nothing.

***

"Wait, wait wait," Darion interrupted, and Gema patiently looked up from the book.

"So the nothing is land, right?"

"Yes, Dare, you're very smart," she said with a smile.

"So this whale is going to try to sink the land into the ocean?" he scoffed. "That's mad.

I thought you said these ancient beasts were intelligent."

Demetri let out a loud, irritated sigh as he looked at Gema, hoping she would agree with his annoyance, but her smiling expression didn't falter.

"Dare, this was a creature who had never, ever encountered anything like land before. Even though you know that you can't make the land sink into the ocean, how would he know that?"

"It's common sense," he said with confidence shining in his blue eyes.

"If you were in the woods," said Gema, "and you saw a piece of land floating in the air, what do you think you would do?"

"But that's impossible. Nothing can just float above the earth like that."

"And to Erulian, anything being above the surface of the ocean was impossible. Now, would you know what to do if you found a patch of land floating in the air?"

Darion fell silent, a bewildered expression on his face, and Gema's eyes returned to the book.

***

Slowly, Erulian turned his massive body
away from the shore and swam out into
the deeper waters, then he turned toward
the nothing--he thrust his body toward
the shore--powerful waves forcing him
forward--swimming as hard as he could,
muscles aching under the strain--faster,
faster--the ocean floor rose closer and closer
to the underside of his body--faster--faster--

His head breached the water's surface as
he felt his stomach scrape against the ocean
floor. He was going too fast--he couldn't
stop--

Suddenly, his whole gigantic body was
completely out of the water, finally sliding to
a painful stop.

The nothing didn't sink. It didn't even
shift.

Fear jolted his nerves as he lay there,
shaking and terrified. With all the force
he could muster, he thrashed this way and
that, trying to push himself back into the
water--but to no avail. Tears streamed down
his face as Erulian laid his massive head on

the dry sand, closed his eyes, and accepted his fate...

Darkness crept onto the land, and the light of the full moon rose over the horizon, dancing elegantly on the water...

From high in the sky, the moon stretched contently and surveyed the earth. Out of the corner of her eye, she spotted a tiny speck outside of the water.

*That's...strange...*she thought to herself as she strained to get a better look.

A great gasp left her mouth at the devastating scene before her eyes. The great Erulian, lying helpless and weak, *outside* of the ocean. The guardian of the water, her eldest and dearest friend, had left his watery home to dire consequences. Tears welled in her eyes as she stared at such a terrible scene.

If he was still alive, there was only one thing that could save Erulian--he had to be returned to the water. The moon closed her eyes, focusing carefully and intently on Earth's mighty force of gravity. She strained and grunted for hours, exhausted, but determined...

As Erulian lay there, breathing weakly, he thought longingly of the creatures still in the water. They would be wondering where he was by then, but they would never be able to find him. He could imagine the search parties wandering the oceans, searching endlessly with hope still in their hearts. They would exhaust themselves, and he knew that they would never give up. Deep pain ached in his massive chest and he knew...he would never see them again. They would never find him lying helplessly outside of the water--how would they even know where to look? And--his heart clenched and broke at the thought of it--who would look after the creatures now? All hope was lost...

Suddenly, the cool ocean waters splashed the tip of his tail, slowly creeping up his body. Surprise jolted him out of his helpless surrender as he looked around, delightfully wondering how this could be possible. He gazed around in every direction, but the only thing he could see was the moon, who gave him an uplifting smile.

Higher and higher the water climbed until Erulian was completely submerged once again, and the cool water soothed his cracking, dry skin. With a swish of his massive tail and immeasurable relief, he broke free of the sand.

Returning to the deeper water, he relished in its soothing, healing touch...but his sadness deepened. The moon's gift may have saved his life, but it did very little to soothe his sorrow. He turned back for last look at the nothing, resting helplessly atop the dark waters, glowing like a ghost in the pale light of the moon. There was no way to sink it, and no way to give the gift of water.

He had failed.

With a heavy heart full of despair, he blew some water out of his blow-hole, ready to take in a massive breath and dive. Tiny water droplets hung in the air all around him...just like before...

He gasped. *That's it...*he thought to himself. *Water...in the air...get water to the nothing...through the air...*

He started swimming as fast as he could in giant, wavy circles. He rocked and jumped, splashing and spraying as much water as he could into the night sky. He splashed and sprayed until the moon bade him farewell and the sun awoke, bright and ready for a new day. Still he splashed and sprayed, his muscles aching, his eyes stinging with fatigue.

Suddenly, the brilliant light of day grew darker and darker, making Erulian stop his mad splashing. Everything around him was shrouded in deep gray... a gray that was not the darkness of the night sky.

Erulian looked up toward the sun. Something high above and gray, almost soft and puffy looking, was blocking its rays... the air felt thick and heavy--and wet. He stared at the gray sky above. Suddenly, light flashed brightly in the sky but was gone in an instant. Powerful booms filled the air and bolts of light flashed over and over again....

Erulian gazed in delight at the first thunderstorm on earth--his plan had worked.

His heart lightened and a smile spread on his giant face as he took in a deep breath, blowing a great gust of wind from his blow-hole. The powerful blast of breath blew the storm until it was directly over the nothing, covering it in a deep shadow. Suddenly, a burst of lightning flashed through the sky, and water began spilling from the storm above. First a trickle, then more--and more--until the air was so thick with water that Erulian could no longer see in front of him.

To Erulian's delight, tiny green sprouts started slowly emerging from the soaked nothing, little living beings that had just been there in the soil, needing that little something extra to help them along--life outside of the water had taken its first few breaths.

He turned away from what was formerly the nothing, tears of joy welling in his eyes, and determination taking over his mind.

After naming the nothing "land", which to him meant "opposite of water", he searched endlessly for more of it. Erulian, the great blue whale of the sea, had a new purpose settle in his steadfast heart--giving life to the land, while guarding the sea.

***

The boys stared in silence at their grandmother. A giant smile spread over Demetri's face, but Darion remained as stoic as ever.

"So not elves or humans," Darion said in a mocking thinking-out-loud sort of way. "The first creature on earth was a giant blue whale. Well I've got to admit, I didn't see that one coming."

"Gema, what kingdom was that from?" asked Demetri in awe, ignoring the sarcastic thoughts from his brother.

"This tale was from the early histories of the Blue Kingdom. Mer Anemos, in elvish of course," Gema answered, and Demetri's eyes were alight with wonder.

"Did all of that *really* happen?" Darion asked, his arms folded over his chest.

"What do you mean?" Gema asked gently.

"Well, that story came from the Blue Kingdom and all, but how do you know it really happened? How do you know you don't have a book of fairy tales or bedtime stories?"

Gema simply stared at him in silence for a moment. Demetri's eyes darted back and forth from the serene face of his grandmother and the sour face of his brother. Amphy's gentle snores filled the silent, slightly tense air. But finally, she spoke.

"I don't."

Darion smiled victoriously and nudged Demetri's arm. "Told you."

"These could be stories," she said, "tales, fantasies, complete fabrications by the imaginations of a few gifted elves. But...they could also be stories rich in deep history. No one was there when the world formed. No one was there to sit with pencil and paper to record the time of the ancient creatures. Anything could have happened. All that matters--is what you believe," Gema closed the book and held it up, the front cover facing the boys.

"This is what the elves believe. These stories speak to their hearts and spirits. They whisper dreams into the ears of elves, dreams that fill them with hope, life, and purpose. These stories could be completely wrong, Darion," she stared deeply into his eyes. "But they could also be right. What matters is not what the story tells, but how it makes you feel. If you are filled with hope and purpose, and you feel your spirit awakening when you hear the words in these tales, that's when you know that you believe."

Darion stared at her, looking as though he had forgotten how to speak. His gaze turned to the snoring fox on the floor, as if he could no longer look Gema in the eye. Demetri could see a rosy flush on Darion's cheeks as his blue eyes stared at Amphy without looking at him. Demetri knew this look of Darion's very well--it was the look on his face when he was lost in his own mind.

"I believe," Demetri whispered. Gema smiled widely.

"I know," she said, her face glowing with warmth. "And now, you boys better go wash up for dinner." Holding the book tenderly in her hand, she slowly got to her feet.

Demetri let out a long, loud moan, wishing he could skip the pointless process of washing himself (he was just going to go and get dirty again tomorrow) and go straight to shoving dinner in his mouth.

"Now now," said Gema sternly but failing to stifle a giggle. "your mother won't let you eat with filthy hands and even filthier bottoms. Just look at your clothes!" She pointed at the mud sliding from their pants down their stools, and neither of the boys could stop themselves from laughing. Darion carefully helped Demetri limp into the house, with Gema right behind them.

Hideaways and Butterflies

A few days later, the sun was high in the sky on a warm afternoon. Demetri and Darion huffed through the woods, both carrying piles of huge sticks in their outstretched arms. Amphy trotted behind them as usual, carrying a stick of his own in his mouth.

"Is...it...much farther?" Darion asked as sweat ran down his forehead.

"I...hope not..." huffed Demetri. "Dad said...southwest...three miles..."

"You're...going north...", Darion said breathlessly.

Demetri drug his feet to a stop and let his logs fall to the ground, putting his hands on his knees to catch his breath. Darion dropped his pile without hesitation and flung himself onto the ground. Amphy sat down beside him, still holding the stick in his mouth and wagging his bushy red tail.

"We've been walking for hours--Couldn't build fort close to home, could you?" Darion said sarcastically, still gasping. "No, it had to be miles and miles--"

"It wouldn't be secret if anyone could find it," Demetri interrupted. "Besides, I never told you that you had to help me."

"It was either come with you or stay home and help Mom clean the house," Darion muttered as he lay flat on his back, looking up through the thick canopy of branches. Barely and sunlight reached the shady forest floor.

Demetri ignored him as he scanned the woods and found a low lying tree branch. He sprinted toward it with a slight limp, still feeling the pain from the thorny branch incident.

"What are you doing?" Darion shouted, still lying comfortably on the ground, but Demetri continued to ignore him as he grabbed the branch and began fearlessly scaling the tree. Darion turned his head just enough to see his brother's feet disappear into the higher branches.

"Oh, great--" Darion shouted as he rolled his eyes. "Excellent idea! Let's have you break your arm while we're lost!"

But Demetri kept climbing.

"You're not going to be able to see anything from up there! You know it's impossible to climb high enough to see through the canopy!" Darion shouted pointlessly, and Demetri still gave no response. Sighing heavily, Darion pulled himself off of the ground and walked toward the tree--the harsh crack of a snapping branch hit his ears, and Demetri's body dropped to the ground right in front of him with a crunching thud.

"Demetri!" Darion screamed in panic as he knelt down before his brother.

"Demetri?" he whispered faintly, worry thick in his voice...

Demetri jolted up, shook his head wildly, and brushed off his shoulders.

"I uh...I found it," he announced awkwardly, slightly out of breath and tenderly rubbing a spot on his arm. Darion's fierce stare could have pierced a hole in Demetri's soul.

"It's not far..." Demetri said in a much smaller voice, but Darion wasn't even blinking.

"Ugh, I'm fine," he insisted as he waved his hand vaguely, trying to dismiss his brother's steely look. "Come on!"

He ran to his pile of sticks, hurled them hastily into his arms, and began sprinting through the shady trees with Amphy frolicking right behind him. Rolling his eyes while another sigh escaped his throat, Darion hurled his sticks into his arms and followed.

Demetri only had to run a short distance before a blinding light suddenly shone into his eyes. He slid to a halt and gazed at a wide, sunny meadow, where the uninterrupted rays of the sun felt warm and comforting on his skin. Thick, emerald green grass filled the open space and felt soft under his bare feet. Flowers of all kinds dotted the meadow with brilliant color, and he deeply breathed in their sweet fragrance. A small, clear pond glimmered near the edge of the meadow, and ducks were contently floating on the surface.

Amphy stopped right in front of Demetri with his teeth still clenched around his stick, panting. As he chuckled at the silly fox, Demetri heard the dragging, heaving footsteps of his twin getting louder, and before he knew it, Darion was gasping for breath right beside him.

"Told you we were going the right way," Demetri said without taking his eyes off of the meadow. "This is the clearing, the one Dad was talking about." He couldn't stop the I-told-you-so smirk from forming on his face.

"Lovely," Darion huffed with a stoic expression. "Can I put these down now?" He asked with a bite in his voice as he looked at the heavy pile of sticks in his arms.

"Oh," said Demetri, "Yeah."

Without another thought, Darion dropped his arms and let his pile of logs fall to the ground right in front of him. Demetri added his to the pile, still moving his head from side to side scanning the meadow, turning his head so far around that he felt like an owl. Amphy trotted confidently over to the pile and dropped his stick on top, his bushy tail flinging happily every which way.

Excitement seared through Demetri's insides at the sight of his new secret hideout, and he jumped gleefully up and down, beaming.

"Haha! We found it! We found it!" he shouted over and over in a singsong voice as he sprinted from one side of the clearing to the other. "We found it! This is going to be the best secret hideout ever! Woohoo!" He spun in huge circles until he was so dizzy that he fell over, rolling around in the soft grass. Despite himself, Darion couldn't help but smile warmly at his brother's delight.

"Well, if we're going to have the best secret hideout ever, we should start building the fort," he said as he jogged over to Demetri and helped him to his feet. "Where's the best place to put it, I wonder...?"

"Over by the water is your smartest move," a deep voice called from behind them. They both turned around to see a tall, burly figure standing in the shadows of the forest.

"Dad!" they shouted together as they ran toward the figure. Dad laughed as he walked, heavy-footed, into the meadow.

"Wow! How did you find us so quickly?" Demetri asked in awe, but Dad just laughed again.

"Quickly? Hah! It took me less than an hour to get here. You two," he knelt down and pointed at them both, "have been gone for five hours. The sun will be setting soon, so it's time to go home and wash up for dinner."

Demetri's heart sank as he let out a moan. "But, Dad, we just got here!"

"You got lost," he said sternly. "You have to take responsibility for your mistakes. So let's go, I don't want to be walking through the woods too close to sunset."

Demetri hung his head and frowned as they shuffled toward the forest. After only two steps, he felt Dad's big, calloused hand on his shoulder.

"Now, now," he said in a much warmer tone, "you always have tomorrow. I'll even take you this time so that you'll know the quickest way to get there. It should have taken you less than an hour, not more than five."

Darion muttered, "told you," elbowing Demetri in the ribs.

Back at the cottage, dinner was served hot and delicious, just as it always was. The boys had eaten more than their fill of roasted deer and hot potato wedges. Amphy had curled up at Darion's feet, plump from the scraps that every member of the family had sneakily fed him.

Their mother busily gathered up the empty plates. She was kind faced woman with rich brown hair and pretty hazel eyes. She wasn't exactly thin but was nowhere near fat, and where the boys clearly didn't get their hair or eyes from her, their faces were both spitting images of hers.

Dad stood and excused himself, kissing Mom tenderly on the cheek as he made his way, exhausted, out of the room. Mom smiled lovingly at his retreating back, and

Demetri and Darion exchanged disgusted looks as they slouched in their seats, comfortably full and sleepy. Gema laughed out loud from her seat.

"So, you found a special spot for your hideout, did you?" she asked, sitting comfortably with her favorite green blanket covering her lap. Demetri and Darion exchanged worried looks, but Gema just chuckled again.

"Don't worry boys. Your secret is safe with me," she winked. Demetri's mouth widened into a toothy smile.

"Yeah, it's a really cool place!" he replied. "It's a huge meadow in the middle of the woods without any trees, but it has a little pond. We're going to build the hideout by the water."

"It sounds like Solaurhia," she said softly, and Demetri jumped upright in his chair.

"Is that an elvish kingdom?" he asked excitedly. "Which one?"

"You would know it as the Yellow Kingdom," she said as she stood gingerly from the table. "Fancy sitting on the porch with an old lady?" she asked with a wink.

Demetri jumped up instantly, but Darion just rolled his eyes and kept his bottom in his seat.

"Darion," Mom said in a sweet voice from the kitchen counter, "you'll be such a great extra set of hands for me if you don't want to keep your grandmother company."

"Ugghhh," Darion grunted, slowly and reluctantly getting out of his seat. After beaming widely at Darion, Demetri skipped merrily to the front porch.

The boys sat on their plain wooden stools and Gema took up her place on the elegant rocking chair with her blanket. She let out a relaxed sigh and stared up toward the sky, fading slowly from sky blue into vibrant orange

"So, Solaurhia? What's it like?" Demetri blurted out quickly. Gema smiled as she contently gazed at the clouds in the distance.

"It's a land of wonder and beauty," she said, barely louder than a whisper. "The emerald meadows stretch out endlessly as far as any eye can see, like an eternal ocean of green. Nothing blocks the brilliant sunlight--no trees, no buildings-- just light that shines with radiating warmth. The grass is as soft as rose petals on weary bare feet. And the flowers…oh my grandchildren, they would take your breath away…they grow in gorgeous patterns that sway in the soft breeze…daffodils, primrose, roses of every color, orchids… even flowers that have no name. They decorate the meadow with patches and lines of brilliant color--with a beautiful blue sky above…"

"It sounds wonderful," whispered Demetri, but Darion slouched in his chair and crossed his arms without saying a word.

"Have *you* ever been there?" Darion asked, eyeballing her suspiciously, but Gema's smile didn't falter as she ignored him.

"Oh, it is a land that has its own special beauty *now*, but it wasn't always like that," she said, looking at Demetri. "It used to be a barren wasteland, with only a few patches of grass and flowers that were miles away from each other."

"What happened?" Demetri asked.

"Well, that's what Solaurhia was like in the early days of Akelian."

"But who fixed it? How?" Demetri pried shamelessly.

Gema grinned and pulled the old, faded elvish book from under her blanket. Demetri's heart lept and he started wriggling excitedly in his seat, but Darion groaned loudly in protest.

"You can always go help your mother, Dare," Gema said quickly, countering his moan as she tied her long hair back. Darion stayed as still as a statue, his arms still crossed. As Demetri watched his brother, he could tell exactly what he was thinking: No matter what kind of story was in that book, it was better than doing stupid chores.

"Now, then..." she said as she carefully opened the book.

***

On a small patch of grass in the middle of nowhere, a teeny gray worm with beady little eyes rested comfortably under a shady flower--a lavender blossom with white tips-- during a brilliantly sunny day. She had minuscule wings that never worked, but she never seemed to mind. In fact, she preferred to do exactly what she was doing: lounging happily and lazily under her flower, cramming blade after juicy blade of grass into her mouth.

Life was peaceful and comfortable for this little insect, called Neryn. Her flower not only offered delicious nectar to drink, but also protection from predators. Nothing ever bothered her, and she was too unremarkable to bother anything. She smiled as she gorged on her grass, knowing she led and enviable existence.

After a while, her throat began to feel extremely dry. Rolling her eyes at the thought of having to move, she slowly rolled over and stretched her brittle legs, preparing for the arduous climb to the top of her flower for some delicious nectar.

Finally, after what seemed like an eternity, she saw the bright, blue sky open up above her as she climbed onto the top of her flower. The warm sun touched her dull gray body and wings, and she closed her eyes as slurped the nectar happily in the warm light.

Then, for the first time in her life, a strange urge nagged at the back of her mind...an urge to look past the grass and flowers to the distant horizon...and as she gave into this strange urge, staring far into the distant horizon...she immediately wished she hadn't.

Her mouth widened in horror and shock; her very breath seemed to be driven from her tiny body. For miles and miles, barren wasteland of brown dirt and mud surrounded her little paradise. Skeletons scarred the land, and haunting echoes floated eerily in the still air. She could almost hear the desperate voices of the dead, the starving, the scared, and the lost...and despite the warmth in the air, a chilling despair filled her soul.

I thought this was paradise... she thought to herself woefully as tears dripped onto her flower...*but it's nothing but a patch of life in a graveyard.*

After a long moment of still silence, she slowly crawled back to the shade and comfort of her home.

Looking around her beautiful paradise, full of greenery, food an life, she felt like she was much more fortunate than she deserved.

If only there were a way to make all of the land as beautiful as my lovely home...

As she pondered, lost in thought, she looked to the stem of her favorite flower. A path of pollen trailed down from the center of the flower, from where she had crawled back to the ground.

An idea struck her as fast as lightning. But could it be done? She was so small and unremarkable...she could never do it alone...

She set out immediately, returning a few hours later with twenty tiny gray worms gathering behind her, all wondering why she called them together. She stood before them in front of her flower, perched on top of a rock, feeling terribly nervous but determined nonetheless.

"My friends...I have seen some terrible and haunting images on this day, and I beg of you to come to the aid of life and land," she announced, hearing the nervous tremble in her voice.

The other worms remained silent; all eyes were fixed on her. She took a few deep breaths to steady herself.

"Has anyone here had the courage to gaze into the distant horizon? Has anyone climbed to the top of the highest grass and peered into the endless beyond?"

A few scattered worms mumbled "I" and nodded their heads, all sharing the same solemn expression.

"For those of you who have, I pity you. For I too have seen the horror that lies beyond the grass. For those of you who have not, feel fortunate that your souls have not had to be tainted. But I will tell you on this day what lies beyond the grass..."

She stared out in front of her, feeling her little heart race as she looked from worm to worm, all staring back at her in suspended silence.

"...Nothing."

They looked around at each other, and Neryn could see the confusion on their faces. The few worms that admitted to seeing the barren land simply stared at the ground beneath their brittle feet.

"The ground is a barren, muddy wasteland even as far as the distant horizon," she continued. "Creatures are starving out there, they are dying...leaving only their bones and desperate souls behind to haunt the land. They starve...while we stuff out bellies here in ignorant comfort." Her voice grew louder and louder, unable to contain her bubbling anger. "They breathe their last, thirsty breaths while we drink nectar until we burst!"

The sea of beady little eyes stared at her, some confused--some horrified--some unsure.

"...But no more," she said with renewed strength replacing the nervous tremble. "There may be a way for us to stop this horror." Turning to the stem of her flower, she pointed to the trail of pollen she had left earlier.

"This pollen holds the key to spreading our oasis through the graveyard. We could carry the pollen on our backs and spread it throughout the empty land. We could plant grass seeds and let the storms nurture them. Do you not see? We could spread our beloved grass all over the land until the emptiness is filled! Together, we can put an end to the suffering!"

***

Darion howled with laughter, making Gema and Demetri both jump in their seats.

"Something funny?" Demetri scowled.

"Well, yeah--a worm is going to go out there and *save the world*--" he said melodramatically, flailing his arms flamboyantly for effect. "These elves sure do have spectacular imaginations."

Demetri folded his arms and grunted loudly, feeling his brows furrow between his eyes. Gema just stared at Darion dreamily.

"Is that hard to believe?" she asked sincerely.

"Oh no, Gema," he said, clearly being sarcastic. "Worms have always been powerful beasts, didn't you know that?"

"Yes I did," Gema said peacefully. Darion abruptly stopped laughing and stared at her a if she had lost her mind.

"...I was joking Gema," he said, sounding as if he were gently speaking to someone who had recently gone mad.

"Oh I wasn't dear," she said. "Never underestimate the ones you perceive as small and weak. Anyone can change the world--they just have to be given the chance."

A twinkle glimmered in her eye as she stared at him, as if waiting for his typical pompous response--but he just stared at her in silence, looking as if he wasn't quite sure what to do with himself.

"Now where were we?" Gema mumbled as she scanned the open page of the book.

***

Neryn stared out at the worms; all was still with silence. To her surprise, they were not cheering or offering themselves to the cause...

They simply stood there in tense, awkward silence. As she stood before them alone, she couldn't help but feel confused and slightly embarrassed.

One word came from the back of the crowd.

"Why?"

Neryn's head was spinning.

"W-What do you mean?" she stuttered.

"Why should we?" The worm asked with a stern eye.

Shaking, she mumbled, "Creatures are suffering--"

"Do you know them?"

"Well...no..."

"So you would have your dear friends live a life of struggle for creatures you have never seen or met?" the stern worm countered. Other worms began mumbling in agreement.

"We are happy, and very fortunate. We shall not give up our blessings for strangers!" a different worm added, shouting.

"There are predators out there!" a female worm called out. "We would be risking our lives!"

"Yes, but--" Neryn tried to counter, but she was drowned out by outraged yelling... the whole crowd was in an uproar.

"The empty lands go on forever. The job would be endless!"

Standing there, completely lost for words with her heart sinking low, all she could do was stare out at her rioting friends, realizing that she was truly seeing them for the first time--a race of selfish, lazy creatures who were more concerned for themselves than the well being of the rest of the world. Her eyes raged with fierce anger as a horrible disgust filled her stomach, leaving a bitter taste in her mouth. She knew in that moment that, if she were to take on this impossible mission, she would be taking it on alone.

Without a second thought, she turned away from the crowd of selfish worms and began to climb her flower. Halfway up the stem, the shouting below subsided--she hesitated for a split second, but continued without looking back down...disgust was all she could feel for them now.

As she piled pollen onto her back, faint mumbling of the crowd below reached her ears--she bitterly wished they would just hurry up and go back home.

Crawling carefully with her back laden with pollen, she descended again on the crowd of worms. Silence had replaced the mumbles as Neryn stopped before them, trying to think of something to say to them. For a while they stared at her heavily burdened, dusty yellow back, and she stared into their empty souls. Fire raged brightly in her eyes, a fire born of anger and determination, coursing through her tiny body, filling her with nothing but the desire to move forward. She crawled through the silent crowd, past the luscious grass, and right to the border of the empty land. Without looking back, she took a deep breath and stepped out into the haunting lands.

For days and days, Neryn left her lavender flower as the light of dawn peered over the horizon, and returned only when the sky turned orange from the setting sun. Every now and then, she would pass another worm when she returned, breathless and exhausted. They would stare at her, some scowling, some confused--a select few wore expressions of guilt and empathy--but she never spoke to them.

A few weeks later, the sun began to rise and the pale light of morning filtered through Neryn's thin eyelids. She opened her eyes and thought fondly of the work that lay ahead of her. She stretched peacefully, ate a few grass blades, and began her crawl to the top of her flower. It was amazing how much easier the crawl had become over the past few weeks. Her little legs and body felt stronger than ever before, and she woke every morning feeling refreshed and exhilarated. Neryn smiled to herself as she piled the day's pollen onto her back and began her crawl back to the haunted land.

"Neryn," a voice called from behind her as she reached the ground. She turned to see the face of the stern worm that had objected and ridiculed her plan so many weeks ago... but his face did not look as stern as it had the last time she saw it. In fact, he seemed almost somber.

"Karo," she replied curtly.

"Listen..." Karo began, but Neryn had already turned away.

"No, wait," he crawled as quickly as he could after her, but she was strikingly fast. "Neryn, Please! Just give me one moment."

She stopped, and Karo crawled furiously to reach her. Clearly, his flaccid body and brittle legs could no longer keep up with Neryn's new strength. Panting and breathless, he finally caught up to her.

"It has been weeks," he said seriously. "You've done enough..."

"No," she interrupted, looking him dead in the eye. "There is still land out there that I have not touched yet."

"Neryn, you could spend the rest of your life doing this, and you would still never finish. You have done more than anyone else would. Is that not enough?"

She said nothing and turned away, refusing to let his words penetrate her mind.

"You cannot save the world Neryn," he insisted.

"I know that," she said, unable to help herself. "But I can help. Sprouts are coming out of the ground where I have sowed."

Karo stared her as if she had just spoken in an unfamiliar tongue.

"Don't you see?" she said, turning to face him. "It's working! At least the land I can touch will thrive. If I can keep one creature from starving...even just one...my life will be worth it."

"But...you don't even know these creatures," mumbled Karo. Rage filled Neryn's tiny body once again.

"How does a chance meeting with me make any one creature more important than another? I have never met our great ancestor, Erulian, but I have met you. Does that make you more important than him?"

Karo stared at the ground, and if Neryn hadn't known better, she would have thought he looked ashamed of himself. She turned her back on him and crawled away toward the empty land.

The next day, Neryn woke to the pale morning sunlight as she always did. She stretched peacefully, enjoyed a quick breakfast, then crawled to the top of her flower to start her daily journey--but as she crawled down to the ground, she gasped in shock...

Dozens and dozens of worms stood before her. They were not gray, stern worms, but smiling yellow ones--yellow with pollen on their backs. Karo crawled from the back of the crowd to face her, his back carrying more pollen than any of the other worms.

"I-I don't--" Neryn stuttered, not believing her eyes.

"We are awaiting your orders, milady," Karo said with a smile, lowering his head in a bow.

Neryn looked from face to kind face, speechless yet again--but this time, it was the kindness of the worms that stole her words. Her heart warmed and tears filled her eyes as she joyfully set them out in all directions toward the empty lands.

With courage battling back the fear in their hearts, the new recruits ventured forward, weighed down and vulnerable toward their new purpose. Neryn felt a rush of affection for her friends return as she continued on her journey with them by her side.

Weeks and weeks went by, and the worms continued sowing the empty lands.

Neryn listened on happily as they shared stories of tiny sprouts, pride ringing in their every word. Neryn knew that they could never cover all of the barren land, but every new blade of grass made it smaller and smaller with each hard day's work.

One fateful day, the sun awoke in a brilliant blaze and stared at down at the land, just as he always did. But this time, something was definitely different. For some strange reason, the brown lands seemed to be turning green--something that had never happened before...

Confused, he peered as close to the ground as he possibly could, and brilliant green grass filled the barren lands for miles and miles. Flowers were blooming and spinning patterns of color into the little sea of green. He laughed out loud with glee and began to wonder where such a miracle came from.

Squinting carefully to get a close look at the ground, he saw tiny, worm-like insects crawling laboriously under the weight of piles of pollen on their frail little bodies. He watched as they journeyed to what remained of the barren lands, spreading pollen and seeds. As he smiled, deeply touched, his heart filled with a warm glow.

This sacrifice must have cost them dearly, he thought to himself. He wondered briefly how he could offer his own services to their cause--and then it hit him.

He closed his eyes with a content smile... glowing drops of sunlight fell rapidly toward the earth, landing like hot wax onto the wings of the worms.

In the barren lands, with pollen still on her back, Neryn stopped instantly as she felt the hot drops spread over her wings. It felt blissful as the bright, glowing drops stretched out and strengthened her wings with radiant light.

As the light of the sun drops began to fade, she stared at her wings with great surprise. Beautiful flowing patterns of lavender, white, and emerald green swirled on her wings--just like the lavender flower that was her home, and the beginning of her journey.

She flapped her new wings with joyful delight--and with each flap they stretched and stretched--growing larger--and larger--swelling and swelling until they were twenty times their old size! As the other worms watched Neryn in awe, they too flapped their wings with a joyful vigor--and they too felt the blissful warmth, strengthening their once brittle wings.

"To the air, my friends! To the air!" Neryn shouted gleefully, flapping her wings as hard as she could as she felt her tiny feet leave the ground for the first time. She looked around and saw her dear friends taking flight with ease.

Flying as high as she could and turning toward the sun, Neryn bowed her head and said a quiet "thank you". Before she turned away, she heard a low, quiet voice that seemed to echo in her mind...

"Flap your wings. Flap them as hard as you can. Close your eyes and flap with all your might," it whispered mysteriously, echoing into the very corners of her mind.

She raised her brilliant new wings high, closed her eyes, and flapped them as hard as she could with one swift motion--to her surprise, a giant gust of air flew from her wings, lifted the pollen from a nearby flower, and carried it far into the horizon.

This simple sight brought tears to her tiny eyes as she finally understood what the sun had given them--the power to create a new force of nature--the wind. They could now spread the emerald grass and beautiful flowers much farther than they ever imagined with incredible ease. They no longer had to choose between living a life of peace or saving the world. Now, thanks to their wonderful gifts, they could have both.

The sun had set them free.

Neryn spread the thrilling news to the rest of her friends, and they perfected their new gifts in no time, ready to continue their loving quest for the life of the land.

Known as Luteala to the elves, and butterflies to humans, the worms happily carry out their work to this day. Whenever you feel a warm gust of wind dancing on your face, you just may have been blessed by the gifts of a butterfly.

***

Gema gingerly closed her book, wearing a tender smile. Demetri's face was alight with wonder.

"Gema, was our hideout meadow made by those butterflies?" he asked excitedly. Darion let out an obvious sigh of annoyance, his arms still folded.

"Give me a break, Tree," he mumbled under his breath, but Gema paid him no mind as she rocked contently in her chair, closing her eyes.

"We're pretty far from Solaurhia," she whispered, and Demetri felt his smile droop into a deep frown.

"But the wind travels farther than any other force in the world," she continued. "It carries storms, birds, pollen--even dreams. Perhaps your clearing did get its start from a very special ancient butterfly." She stopped rocking and leaned forward until she was nose to nose with Demetri, her aged eyes wide and staring deeply into his.

"This is one of the most important things I will ever tell you, grandson--so pay close attention," she whispered through a stern expression. Demetri gulped and held his breath, waiting.

"Never, ever, say that something is impossible," she finally said.

She stared deeply into his eyes for a very long second, as if engraving the message into his soul--then smiled widely and resumed her peaceful rocking. Demetri blinked and turned to look at his brother, whose arms were no longer crossed as he looked back at him.

"Yeah, we know. Anything is possible blah blah blah. We've heard that a hundred times," scoffed Darion.

"Oh no, plenty of things are impossible," she smiled mischievously.

"...What?"

"Never say that something is impossible. The only thing that makes something impossible...is *saying* that it is."

The boys looked at each other, utterly confused.

"So you're saying that I can change the color of the sky if I wanted to?" Darion asked.

"That's ambitious, but yes."

"But that's impossible."

"Now it is, yes," her mischievous smile spread from ear to ear. Demetri's face was beaming, but Darion was perplexed.

"Now then," Gema chimed, "if you two want to build your fort tomorrow, I suggest getting to bed early. We're almost out of daylight anyway." She motioned toward the brilliant red light underneath the steadily darkening sky. "Your father will be up with the sun and if you aren't awake as well, I'm quite sure you will lose your guide."

The boys let out an identical moan.

"Well, I guess it's worth it," said Darion with a sigh. "It's definitely better than getting lost in the woods for hours again."

"Har Har," Demetri rolled his eyes. "And it will give us more time to build the fort!" He jumped to his feet, nearly falling over in his haste. Gema just laughed.

"You boys give your Gema a kiss before you head in the house," she said with a warm smile wrinkling up her face. Both boys kissed their grandmother on the cheek, said goodnight with wide smiles, and headed through the front door, stretching and yawning all the way to their bedroom.

The Stag of Seasons

Demetri was lying comfortably in his bed when the rising sun shone red through his closed eyelids. *Stupid sun*, he thought to himself without opening his eyes. Trying to drift off again, he rolled over to face the wall, covering his head with his soft, fluffy blanket.

"Don't even think about it," Darion's cool voice rang out from across the room. Demetri groaned loudly in protest.

"Noooo...I'll be useless today...just ten more minutes."

"Not useless, just lazy," said Darion, and Demetri swore he could hear his brother rolling his eyes. "Now get up. You have to help Mom with the chores today, too."

Another defiant moan rolled out of Demetri's throat.

"Don't make me sic Amphy on you," Darion warned him.

"Ugh, fine." With another pointedly loud yawn and stretch, he gave in and opened his eyes, finding Darion standing just at the foot of his bed, wearing a worn down pair of pants and clearly half-way through getting dressed.

"And just so you know, there's nothing threatening about a lick attack from your fox," Demetri added.

"You got up, didn't you?" Darion quickly retorted as he rummaged through his wooden chest full of clothes. "And he's your fox, too."

Amphy hopped down from his favorite little nest--the end of Darion's bed. Demetri finally set his feet on the floor as he watched Amphy trot to the door and sit, statue like, waiting for Darion to take him outside.

My fox too, eh? Demetri thought to himself, watching Darion smile broadly as he pet "their" fox on the head with one hand while forcing the other hand through the sleeve of his shirt. Amphy panted loudly, wagging his fluffy tail.

Though Darion was the one who found the injured Amphy when he was just a little pup, the whole family had insisted that the fox was a special friend for both of the twins. This was a great idea in theory, but Amphy followed Darion around like a--well, like a lost little puppy.

With irksome dread already flooding his mind, Demetri began looking for an old shirt and pair of pants, ones that he didn't mind getting soap, fox poo, or whatever else he was bound to get covered in while doing chores. He sighed as he pulled his shirt over head. *What a waste*, he thought bitterly. *I could be working on the hideout, but that's not important to Mom and Dad, apparently. It's not like we have much more summer left.*

"We can go work on the hideout if we finish early," said Darion without looking up from tying his sandals, almost as if he could read his mind. Ignoring the eerie timing of his brother's comment, Demetri jumped up and down with excitement, thinking that there may be a ray of sunshine at the end of this gloomy day of work after all.

"You really think so?" he squeaked gleefully. "Do we have a lot to do? How long do you think it will take? What do we have to do? Do you think--"

"I don't have a clue," Darion interrupted coolly. "Let's get this over with."

They met Mom in the small clearing in the front of the cottage. Covered in dirt and holding a shovel, she wiped the sweat from her forehead as she surveyed a soft, freshly dug patch of dirt. Demetri and Darion exchanged woeful glances.

"Oh, good," Mom breathed as she picked up another shovel and shoved them into the boys' arms. "I want six square feet dug up right here. Make sure the earth is good and soft."

"Why?" Darion asked defiantly. "We already have a garden in the back."

"I'm going to grow berries. We need more fruit in our diets," she said as she brushed the dirt off of her hands and legs.

"Isn't it a little late in the season to--"

"I'm preparing for next year," she snapped. Clearly, Mom was feeling a bit overwhelmed today--and an overwhelmed Mom was a grumpy Mom.

"Now, you two get to work or you won't get any delicious berry cobbler when the berries come in. Meet me inside when you're done."

The boys both sighed as she walked away, and began attacking the ground with their shovels. Within minutes, Demetri was already pouring with sweat, ready for this arduous task to be over with. *If we were at the hideout, we could just take a dip in the pond*, he thought to himself bitterly as he forced the shovel into the relentless soil over and over again, and each stroke was harder than the last.

Two grueling hours later, the filthy twins shuffled back to the cottage, holding their shovels against their shoulders.

"Do you think we still have time to go work on the hideout?" Demetri asked hopefully.

"Oh, definitely," said Darion with a smile through the dirt threatening to hide his face. "The sun is nowhere near its highest point in the sky yet."

Demetri beamed with hopeful delight. They shuffled into the cottage with extreme care not to track dirt onto the floor and possibly create more work for themselves. Footsteps were echoing through the hallway from the kitchen, so they made their way down and through the only hallway in the cottage. Mom was adding filthy rags mountainous pile of dirty laundry in front of her.

"We're done with the garden," said Demetri, barely masking his anticipation to be told those four simple words--You're free to go.

But that's not what Mom had to say.

"Oh, thank goodness," she said without looking at them as she walked out of the room. The boys exchanged looks of confusion, but when Mom returned, their confusion was quickly replaced with dread.

It was looking like Demetri wasn't going to hear his four words, because underneath each of Mom's arms was a bucket--a gigantic, monster of a bucket that Demetri could easily sit in with room to spare. Which could only mean--

"Here," Mom said as she dropped the buckets onto the floor with a loud clang. "Go to the river and get me come clean water."

"But Mom! That will take forever!" Demetri protested with a slight whine.

"You are supposed to be helping me with the chores today, young man!" she barked back with impressive volume. Darion looked at Demetri with an intense keep-your-mouth-shut expression on his face, but Mom closed her eyes, took a deep breath, and forced a patient smile.

"Your father has fallen ill and can't help me today. There simply isn't enough time in the day for me to do everything your Dad needs to do on top of everything that I need to do. I need you two to stand up and help me out in a big, big way today. Can you do that for me?"

How in Akelian could they resist? Demetri gave her a weak smile and nodded in agreement, and Darion did the same. Frustration was still bubbling hot in Demetri's gut, only now he felt guilty for it.

They picked up their massive buckets and headed for the river, feeling slightly defeated. After a 15 minute walk to the water with their empty buckets under their arms, and a 55 minute walk back dragging their full buckets behind them, they had finally reached the clearing behind the cottage where Mom always did the laundry. Sweating and huffing, Demetri and Darion stopped just short of the laundry spot, panting.

"That didn't take too long, did it?" Demetri said breathlessly.

"No...not...too long..." said Darion, still trying to catch his breath.

"We should still have time to go to the hideout, right?"

"Probably..... it took...less time....to get the water...than I thought it would."

"This is great!" Demetri said excitedly. "I want to put a rope ladder to get from the first floor to the second floor. And we need to work on the rails so that we don't...fall..."

At that exact moment, a red furry blob came pelting toward the boys. Hopping gleefully along the way, Amphy darted at lightning speed--right toward the clean water...

"No--no no NO!! Amphy! STOP!" Demetri yelled, flailing his arms madly in front of him--but to no avail. Amphy sped right through Demetri's legs with powerful force, knocking him face first into his bucket of clean water. Sputtering, Demetri pulled himself out of the frigid water to find Amphy sitting in Darion's full bucket, wagging his sodden tail and flinging water everywhere, a rabbit hanging from his mouth.

Demetri shot a sharp look at Darion, but Darion simply sighed.

"I guess he was hot," he said, "Or he thinks I'm hungry."

"This isn't funny!" shouted Demetri, ringing the water out of his sandy blond hair. "We have to go back and get more water, don't we?"

"Beyond any doubt. Mom won't use water that a fox sat in to wash clothes--or to do anything for that matter."

Demetri grunted as he tipped his bucket over, dumping the rest of the unusable water out, and Darion followed suit. Amphy splashed in Demetri's puddle, chasing his tail in wild circles with the rabbit still clamped in his jaws.

"Come on," said Darion as he picked up his empty bucket. "Let's get this over with."

Just as Demetri took his first step, Amphy shook out his fur wildly, spraying both of the boys in drops of mud. Without saying a word (but making sure to stare daggers into Darion's eyes), Demetri picked up his bucket, spat the mud out of his mouth, and stomped toward the river.

A full 90 minutes later, the sodden and sluggish twins slumped into the kitchen where Mom was hovering busily over the counter, which was covered in a thick layer of flour.

"Did you boys get the water for me?" she asked without looking up.

"Yes, Momma," they both said in a monotone voice. Darion leaned over a chair to sit down and rest for just a moment--

"Don't you DARE sit on my chairs covered in all that mud!" Mom shouted, some stray hairs falling out of her plait and into her face. She had just happened to turn and see the filthy boys just seconds before Darion's bottom hit the seat. "What in Akelian happened to you two?"

"Long story," said Darion, standing up and leaning on the wall for support. Mom shot him a steely look, but he didn't move.

"What are you making?" Demetri asked brightly, trying to divert her attention from his rebellious brother. She turned back to the counter, her hands busily moving again.

"It's a meat pie," she said. "It's full of fat and nutrients that your father needs right now. Not to mention it's Gema's favorite.

"You mean your pheasant pie?" asked Demetri hopefully, salivating. Mom's pheasant pie was his favorite as well.

"Yes, honey," Mom said. Demetri couldn't see her face, but he could tell she was smiling and possibly blushing.

"With carrots?"

"Yes."

"And mushrooms?"

"Yep."

"And--"

"It looks messy," Darion interrupted. Demetri glanced at the flour covering the counter and falling onto the floor, and his stomach fell.

"Too messy," he agreed.

"And flour is--"

"--really hard to clean..."

"Put a lid on it, you two," Mom snapped. "I'm not going to make you clean it."

"Oh," said Darion as both boys breathed a sigh of relief.

"You're going to be doing the laundry," she said, without turning to see the appalled look on their faces; their jaws nearly hit the floor.

"What?!" shouted Demetri.

"But we've never done laundry before," said Darion, sounding slightly bewildered.

"That's gonna take forever!" Demetri whined loudly.

Mom turned to face them, that steely look in her eyes once again. "There is no better time to learn. I need to be free to make the pies for tonight, which means the laundry falls on you two. Now I don't want to hear another word about it. Go."

There was no point in arguing. Laundry normally took Mom a long time to do, but she was also an expert. Demetri couldn't even imagine how long it would take them. If they finished before the sun set, he would be surprised--and there was no chance of working on the hideout after nightfall.

For some strange reason that the boys did not fully understand, they were not allowed to leave the cottage after the sun had completely set. Gema always said, "Never cross the forest at night, lest your worst fears come to light," whatever that meant.

Demetri sighed and began throwing filthy rags into the big wicker basket that he always saw Mom use for the laundry.

Once every soiled and smelly piece of linen in the cottage was finally in the basket, forming a towering pile that extended much higher than the sides of the basket itself, each of the boys grabbed a handle and hobbled into the clearing in the back yard. Fortunately, Amphy was nowhere to be found, and the water in the buckets was just as clear and clean as it had been when they dropped it off.

"Do you think we'll still have time?" Demetri asked with no real hope.

"Maybe...if we hurry," Darion mumbled, his blue eyes already focused on sorting the clothes.

After smiling weakly at his brother, Demetri sighed and threw a filthy rag into the bucket with the washboard, hopelessness filling his veins. He could practically feel the day slipping away from him.

Three brutal hours later, the twins stood back and stared at the clothesline, covered with damp but pristine clothes and sheets, swaying slightly in the warm breeze. Demetri couldn't help but smile with pride as he clapped his brother on the shoulder.

"Shall we go find Mom?" he asked gleefully.

"Oh, we shall," Darion said, trying to hide a prideful smile.

Exhausted, filthy, and smelly, they staggered back into the kitchen. The enticing smell of sizzling meat and savory sauce wafted through the air, and both boys inhaled deeply through the nose, drinking in the delicious aroma with their mouths salivating--but Mom wasn't there. They looked around the hallway, walked into the living room, and peered out the window into the front clearing, but there was no disheveled Mom busily working away.

"Oh, don't worry boys," Gema's soft, crackling voice fluttered behind them from the kitchen. "Your mother is in the back, caring for your father."

"Is he feeling better?" Darion asked as they boys made their way back toward the kitchen and the delicious scent.

"Oh, yes," Gema said with a grunt, slowly lowering herself into her kitchen chair. "He'll be right as rain in no time. Your mother has already sliced up the pheasant pie, so be a dear and grab your poor Gema a plate."

"Poor Gema my rear," said Darion with a playful smirk. "Feeling a little lazy today, are we?"

Gema chortled as she watched Darion grab her a nice big slice and set it in front of her. Demetri quickly grabbed his own plate and sat down as well. Though he loved pheasant pie, he was much more interested in getting to the hideout as quickly as he could.

"Did--" he hesitated. "Did Mom give you any more chores for us to do?"

"No," she smiled, stabbing her pie with a fork. "I believe you are both free for the day."

"Woohoo!" Demetri shouted, jumping out of his seat with delight, his pie forgotten.

"Come on, Darion!" he said joyfully as he grabbed his brother's arm. "We can work on the rope ladder and the swinging ropes with the--"

"Demetri, you can't go to the hideout today. Not at this hour," said Gema.

His stomach plummeted. It felt as if someone had punctured his swelling heart with a sewing needle.

"Why not?" he moaned. "We worked really hard today."

"By the time you reach it, the sun will have set. You would have to make the return journey in the dark, and as you know--"

"Never cross the forest at night, lest your worst fears come to light," he recited gloomily, slumping back down onto his seat. He had spent all day doing back breaking chores, was nearly drowned by a fox, and now he couldn't even go to his favorite place in the world, the one thing that he had been looking forward to all day. He had never felt so miserable.

Stupid sun, with its setting at night and what not, he thought to himself as Gema and Darion stuffed their faces, but he had completely lost his appetite. *Why does the sun have to go down so soon? And why is it going down sooner all of a sudden?*

"Gema," he said out loud, trying not to sound too grumpy. With her head leaned into her pie and her mouth still full, she mumbled something unintelligible.

"Why is the sun setting so soon now?" he asked.

"Beekauv aurum ish kumin," she said through mouthfuls of food, still chewing sloppily.

"Come again?" Darion snickered. Gema swallowed loudly.

"Because autumn is coming--well, that's what I was trying to say at least, but I seem to have failed miserably," she turned to Darion with a wink, and her mischievous smile spread from ear to ear. Demetri, however, was finding it difficult to feel so light hearted after such a rough day.

"I wish there was no autumn," he mumbled into his uneaten pie. "And why do we need stupid winter anyway? There's no food and it's always too cold to go anywhere. It doesn't make sense. I wish it could be summer all year long."

"Oh, you don't want to wish for that," Gema said vaguely, barely paying attention to him. "Heavens me! My plate is empty and my belly is full. I do believe today would be a great day to sit on the porch and watch the sun set."

She slowly got to her feet, her long hair falling down to the floor, and shuffled down the hallway. For a few moments, the only sound that could be heard was the clanging of Darion's fork on his plate as he too finished his pie.

Gema poked her head into the kitchen doorway as Darion cleared the table, leaving Demetri's plate where it was.

"Fancy joining an old lady for a spectacular sunset?" she said with a wink.

Demetri was feeling far too resentful toward the sun to see the beauty in it setting. He had sunk further into his chair with no intention to move even an inch, but something old and faded in Gema's hand happened to catch his eye.

"The book!" he grinned and sprang up, knocking his chair over with a clang. "Yes my lady, I would be honored to escort you to the porch." He bowed low, then lifted his head and beamed at her.

"Will you be joining us, young sir?" asked Gema, looking at Darion.

"Oh yeah," he said sarcastically. "I'm brimming with joy over more elvish tales. No thanks. I think I'll play with Amphy for a while."

All three of them turned to look at Amphy. He was lying in the corner of the kitchen on is back, tongue hanging out of his mouth, with his feet twitching in the air. Demetri couldn't suppress his giggles.

"He must be dreaming about more rabbits--I can tell you guys are going to be thoroughly entertained," he said mockingly, but Darion just rolled his eyes.

"Fine," he conceded. "I guess one more story wouldn't hurt."

"I think you love them and just refuse to admit it," said Demetri teasingly as they all made their way to the front porch.

"Oh, definitely. I can barely contain my enthusiasm."

The porch was radiant with brilliant red light, shining throughout the entire clearing and giving the tops of the trees the appearance of being on fire. A crisp breeze blew gently past them, carrying the scent of a cool night at the end of a long summer day. All three of them sat down and stared peacefully into their clearing, which was alight with glowing fireflies. Demetri could just make out some deer right behind the tree line, grazing on the grass and bushes. Some of the stars were beginning to shine up above, while most remained invisible, waiting for the inky night sky to come out and play.

"What a beautiful evening," Gema said serenely as everyone took their normal seats.

"See?" said Demetri. "Wouldn't it be great if we could have nights like this all year round? No one needs the stupid winter."

"Oh, my dear Tree, you couldn't be more wrong," she said as she opened the book. Anticipation grew in Demetri's chest as a smile spread on his face.

"Is this one really long?" Darion asked. "Just curious-- sunset and all--"

But Gema just ignored him.

"The story I am going to tell you comes from the high cliffs and forests of Aleodyn, the Green Kingdom. This is a tale of the world almost exactly as you wish it to be, Tree. For part of the world is bathed in the constant sunlight of summer, while the other part is blanketed eternally by the snows of frosty winter. The seasons never change, and never touch each other..."

Even Darion couldn't hide his interest.

***

It was a particularly freezing day in a particularly freezing wood, but such was normal in this forever frigid forest. There were very few animals that lived here, but they were accustomed to the constant fall of snow, the steely cold grounds, and the eerie silences that stretched into every corner of their home. In fact, there was only one animal who even dared to roam around in the biting open air.

Endlessly wandering and surveying his hostile home, a stag of great majesty and wisdom stood watch, braving the cold so that others did not need to. Every day was the same: wander through the cold and look for creatures that may need his help, yet every day he found no one, for they all slept in nests or caves or underground holes, hidden and safe from the hostility above...but this was no ordinary day. This was the day that would change the stag's life, and the world, forever.

The stag, called Paleo, was wandering through the freshly fallen snow. The sky was deep, smoky gray, as always. The lands were as lifeless as cold stone...as they were every day. Yet, despite the empty lands, a faint noise floated through the trees behind him, one that he could not quite identify. Pricking up his ears, he turned his head, but stood as still as a tree with no wind. Silence had fallen all around him once again, but he dared not move. The noise echoed through the trees once again, but this time, he knew what it was--a growl. With his heart pounding furiously in his chest, he lowered his head, ready to show his massive antlers to whatever beast made such a noise.

The growl was dangerously close now, but somehow, it did not sound as threatening as he thought it had before. In fact, it did not sound threatening at all. It was a weak whimper, as though from a frightened creature. Bewildered by the mystery of this noise, he raised his head once again. Through heavily falling snow, Paleo could just make out a large silhouette in the distance, slowly growing nearer. Though he was unsure why he was doing so, he carefully made his way toward it...after just a few short steps, three smaller silhouettes came bounding into view.

"Help...me...please..." said the large figure as it collapsed heavily onto the snow covered ground, the smaller figures still bounding around. Paleo sprinted forward.

A black bear lay shivering and weak on the cold ground, while three small cubs continued to frolic all around her. Deep sadness and worry had worn lines on her sunken face. Though her black fur was thick, she was badly emaciated. Paleo began to worry that she would draw her last breath right in front of his eyes.

He turned to look at the cubs. They were the likeness of their mother, but their fur was much silkier and thicker. These were three very fat, healthy cubs full of energy. Deep compassion filled Paleo's heart as he realized what he was witnessing. Mother Bear had given her cubs everything she had to keep them healthy, sacrificing her own health to keep them alive and well. Blinking back tears, he spoke gently and peacefully to her.

"Please rest, Mother Bear," he said as she gasped a painful breath. The cubs were playing merrily around the trunk of an evergreen tree, yelping joyfully, and a pained smile spread on Mother Bear's face as she watched them through sunken eyes.

"Please...my cubs...help them..." she whispered weakly. Paleo laid beside her, lowering his head to hear her. "I...have no milk...to feed them...please..."

Paleo stared at her in wonder. Mother Bear lay with death whispering into her very ear, and all she asked for was food for her cubs.

With an admiring smile, Paleo quickly rubbed his head beside hers in a loving embrace. With his quick farewell, he sprang to his feet and dashed into the shadows of the snow storm. Running as fast as he could, he scanned the lands all around him, praying for some sort of food. He ran and ran with all of the might and power that he could muster, the trees and the snow passing by in a flash.

Suddenly, his front legs crashed into something hard, and his face fell forward straight into the snow. Shaking his head and sputtering, he looked around to find the body of a caribou. Whether it perished from starvation or the freezing cold, he did not know...but he knew that he had found what he was looking for. As carefully and respectfully as he could, he dragged the caribou back through the darkness of the woods to the giant evergreen tree.

When he finally returned, a horrible sight burned into his eyes. Mother Bear was lying completely still--and lifeless. The cubs were huddled together against her massive body, trying to gather warmth from the mother that he feared was no longer with them. His eyes began to well with tears and a terrible ache entered his heart, a fierce pain that he had never felt before.

He was too late.

Knowing that the cubs still needed nourishment, he dragged the caribou as close to them as possible. He hoped that, at the very least, the cubs were old enough to know how to eat meat. To his delight, the cubs jumped toward the caribou and began to take tiny bites of the frozen flesh. Paleo smiled at the sight as he rubbed his head against Mother Bear's one more time. He only wished he could have saved her too.

Suddenly, the vast body of mother bear took in a deep breath, making Paleo gasp in shock as she opened her weak eyes and smiled gratefully. With tears still flowing, he smiled gently back at her. She shakily nibbled on the caribou, filling her belly with as much meat as she could. She would be able to make milk again soon--she could feed her cubs, and they would all survive...for now. He beamed at her as he watched her slowly regain her strength, but a sense of foreboding felt thick in his mind, one that he could not shake.

There was no alternative: he had to journey in search of food for his people. He could not let this happen again to mother bear...or to anyone. After drawing a deep breath of determination, he turned to Mother Bear.

"Look for me. I know not where I am going, nor for how long I will be gone. But look for my return. If you are ever starving and afraid, think of me, and I will give you hope. For when I return, no animal will ever feel the pain of hunger again. You have my word."

With these final words of farewell, Paleo bowed his impressive head low, turned away, and dashed out of sight.

***

"Uh, Gema..." Darion whispered.

"Paleo searched and searched for many days..."

"Gema," he tried again.

"but for what, he did not know..."

"GEMA!" he shouted, making both Gema and Demetri jump slightly.

"Sunset," he said simply, and Demetri looked at the sky to see that Darion was right. Only the tiniest bit of reddish glow clung to the horizon.

"Oh, right," said Gema, slowly rising from her rocking chair. "Better finish this inside then."

Demetri took one last long look at the sky before shuffling through the front door, closing it reluctantly behind him.

"Man, I sure wish we could see what this place looks like at night. I mean, we have a mystery right outside our front door! *Why* can't we go out at night?" he wondered aloud, but Gema simply waved her hand dismissively as she took up her favorite chair by the living room fireplace.

"I'll tell you when you're older," she said as she opened the book again. Demetri sighed and sat in the floor on the rug beside Darion.

"Okay, here we go: 'Knowing that the cubs still needed nourishment, he dragged the caribou--'"

"We're further along than that," Demetri interrupted with a smile.

"Oh, I'm sorry dear. The mind of old age," she giggled, but Darion rolled his eyes.

"Let's *not* make this any longer than it needs to be," he moaned, but Demetri shot him a piercing look.

"Feel free to go," said Gema peacefully, "I'm sure your mother still has plenty of chores you could be helping her with."

"What a lovely story this has been!" said Darion through clearly forced enthusiasm. "I wonder what will happen next? Do tell, Gema!"

Everyone laughed as Gema scanned the page for her place.

"Ah. There we are. 'There was no alternative: he had to journey in search of food--'"

"Try again," said Demetri with a patient smile.

"Goodness me," she mumbled, running her finger down the page. "Ah!"

***

Paleo searched and searched for many days, but for what, he did not know. Perhaps there was food underground for his people. Maybe some sort of strange, underground forest was fed by just a few beams of sunlight peering through tiny holes in the ground above it. Perhaps a cave held new vegetation for them to feast on? Any food would have to be sheltered from the bitter cold and frost bitten ground, so he wandered aimlessly, searching for the entrance to some sort of tunnel or massive cave. Yet, after nearly a month of fruitless searching, he began to wonder if he had chosen an impossible mission.

Dreading the thought of returning empty handed, he began to prepare himself for his long journey home--a journey of defeat.

Yet, as he looked into the distant horizon, a strange sight met his eyes. The snow seemed to have turned a vibrant shade of green. Could exhaustion be playing tricks on his mind?

Curiosity winning over the heaviness of defeat, he carefully lurked toward the horizon, inching closer and closer, until he was just a step away from another world.

What is this strange land? he thought to himself as he bravely stepped over the threshold. Suddenly, his hooves felt something they had never felt before: soft, radiating warmth. Strange, soft, emerald plants were growing in long strands out of the ground. Cautiously, he lowered his head and nibbled on some of them--to his delight, they were refreshing and delicious, and he couldn't help but beam as he looked around, seeing this unusual plant growing in fields all throughout this strange land.

The trees were not the barren skeletons of his home world, but were alive with vibrant leaves in every shade of green. Some even had little groups of gorgeous, tender leaves of pink, blue, orange, and every other color. Their enticing sweet fragrance floated throughout the lands, perfuming every tree and bush. Though these particular leaves did seem to attract a great deal of insects, they were sweet and juicy, and he hungrily sampled every kind he could find.

After a hearty meal of these exotic foods, Paleo wandered the lands contently with a full stomach, something he had never experienced before. As he drifted lazily through the lands, he saw chipmunks dashing around swiftly through tree trunks. Squirrels were jumping fearlessly from tree to tree, birds were singing merrily from branches high above him, and bizarre, scaly creatures with long tongues and tails rested on rocks, bathing in the warm sunlight.

Never before had he seen so many creatures out in the open, yet what amazed him most was the sky. Accustomed to the stone gray skies of his world, he never knew that the sky could be so vivid and blue. White, puffy things seemed to be stuck up there, floating slowly and gently in the breeze.

He had so many questions about this bizarre new world that his head threatened to explode.

Wandering through a small clearing, he stumbled across a bush full of little red and black circles. He stared at them intently, wondering whether or not they were edible, when a silvery voice shimmered from behind him.

"You should not eat those."

Paleo sharply turned his head, and his heart began to hammer faster than a hummingbird's. A doe stood before him with a sweet smile and enchanting eyes. Her silky, chestnut fur shined in the sunlight, giving her a radiant glow. Stunned by her incredible beauty, Paleo was breathless and his feet had stopped working.

"I have been watching you," she said, her voice more captivating and beautiful than the sweetest melodies of songbirds. Awestruck, Paleo seemed to have lost his own voice.

"You look upon the grass and trees as if you have never seen them before. Am I right to assume that you are a stranger to these woods?" she asked with an intoxicating smile, but something she said seemed to give Paleo back his voice.

"...Grass?"

"Yes," she said patiently.

"Forgive my ignorance, my lady, for I am a stranger here as you rightfully guessed. What is this...grass?"

The doe smiled, bent her head low, and nibbled the strange green plants he had enjoyed earlier.

"This is grass," she said as she lifted her head. "That is the name given to the small plants that cover most of the ground."

Paleo burned with excitement as he frolicked to a nearby tree, pointing his nose toward some of the tender pink leaves that had such a wonderful fragrance.

"What are these curious leaves called?" he asked, now hungry for knowledge of this new world. The doe simply smiled kindly.

"They are flowers. They grow in every color you could possibly think of, and some have many colors. Their alluring fragrance attracts insects that help more flowers grow." She smiled and breathed in deeply, drinking in the sweet fragrance.

"I am named for the flowers, so I have a special connection with them. The creatures here call me Floryn, the Doe of Spring." Fluttering her eyes, she turned to look at him. "What do the creatures call you?"

What was this strange feeling? His heart seemed to be swelling, full to the brim with intense warmth and emotion. Every time he looked at this beautiful doe, called Floryn, he felt as though his heart was trying to pull him closer to her.

"I am Paleo, the Stag of Winter, or so I am called by the creatures of my home land," he said, a slight nervousness in his voice. What magical power did Floryn have over him? He had never felt this way before, yet despite the unfamiliarity and the confusion, he found that he loved it. Despite the fear laced into his feelings of unimaginable joy, he adored this new feeling as much as he adored this wonderful doe.

"Winter?" She pondered. "What is winter?"

Paleo smiled as they trotted along, side by side, telling each other of the wonders of their own worlds.

***

"Wait, wait, wait," Darion interrupted with a skeptic tone, holding a mug of fresh, hot tea that Mom had brought each of them. "So you mean to tell me that two deer, the mindless rats with hooves that poop all over our clearing and eat our crops just fell in *love*?"

"Anything is possible, Dare," Gema said gently. "Remember, these stories are from ancient times. Who knows what kind of strange phenomena happened back then."

But Darion just snickered. "What a load of flapdoodle."

After nearly spitting out his tea, Demetri swallowed quickly and howled with laughter.

"Flapdoodle?!" he finally managed to say, holding his sides from laughing so hard.

"Yeah," said Darion, folding his arms. "Problem?"

"Is that even a word?" Demetri teased, suppressing another fit of giggles.

"Of course it's a word! It means 'nonsense'!" Darion shouted defiantly, but Demetri couldn't stop his hysteric laughter. Darion just sat there, arms crossed, waiting for his brother's laughing fit to be over with. Gema's eyes bounced awkwardly between her two grandsons as Demetri finally started to catch his breath.

"Sorry Dare. That's just...the funniest word I've ever...FLAPDOODLE!" he laughed heartily, rolling over from side to side on the couch while clutching his aching sides.

"You're a sack of flapdoodle," Darion spat.

"Hey!" Demetri shouted, his giggles ceasing immediately.

"See? You reacted. Definitely a word," said Darion smoothly with a smug smile. Demetri opened his mouth to retort, but Gema interrupted him.

"Shall we continue?" she said patiently, her finger holding her place in the book. Both boys stared daggers into each other, but nodded their heads.

"Now, then..."

***

The doe and stag wandered peacefully for quite some time, but Paleo knew not for how long. It could have been hours, days, or even weeks, and he would not have known. In the presence of Floryn and her lovely tales of spring, even time seemed to have frozen.

Suddenly, as they trotted alongside a babbling brook, a gray rabbit hopped out of a large nearby bush. The deer both stopped abruptly, noticing the pained worry in his eyes.

"Please...I need...Doe of spring...I need..." he stammered heavily, threatening to succumb to panic. "I need your help. I...

need....it's just...no words can tell..." His voice broke with the last words, and he disappeared into the bush again. After exchanging worried glances, both deer carefully pushed their heads into the bush.

Concealed underneath the vegetation were five tiny bunnies and one mother rabbit. The mother was well fed and healthy, but tears streamed down her face as she gazed upon her children. Every single one of them lay on the ground, shaky and breathless, with only the energy for weak moans of pain that could barely be heard. The mother stared desperately at Floryn.

"We cannot find any food for them that isn't riddled with insects," she cried. "The plagues are destroying all of our food, and our babies are becoming more ill by the moment. Please help us."

After a moment's thoughtful silence, Floryn bowed her head and gave the mother a reassuring smile.

"Look for me," she said. "I know not where I am going, nor for how long I will be gone. But look for my return. If you are either ill or afraid, think of me, and I will give you hope. For when I return, no creature will ever suffer the pain of illness and plague again. You have my word."

With that last farewell, the two deer departed. Paleo was ready and eager to help as he galloped along the riverbank, but he was not sure he fully understood.

"If the mother and father eat the same food as the children, why are only the children falling so gravely ill?--Floryn?"

He turned to see her trotting sadly behind him, her head hung low in despair. He stopped and waited for her to catch up with him, wondering why she seemed to be in no rush to find help for those poor bunnies.

"The adult creatures in this forest can stomach the insect-infested foods," she said gravely. "Their stomachs are older and stronger. But the children...most children do not survive long enough for their stomachs to become strong enough." Her voice was barely more than a whisper and began to break. "The children of my world are dying... and there is nothing I can do to stop it."

They continued to wander mournfully, but after only a few silent moments, Floryn simply stopped. There was no reason to continue, for there was nothing to be done. Paleo wished to comfort her, but he knew his words would be no more help to her than to the dying bunnies back in the bush.

This new world was full of beauty, warmth, and color. Yet, even with this exotic wonder, Paleo could not help but miss his own lands. Yes, his people were suffering as well, but the children--the children never suffered this type of pain--at least in winter the children were safe--

The thought hit him harder than a bolt of lightning. Without another word, he placed his front legs together, held his head toward the sky, and closed his eyes--letting his mind clear and fill with icy, frozen thoughts--

The clear blue skies above slowly fell to a deep gray all around them, and the warm air suddenly held a biting chill in its wind. Giant flakes of snow fell from the gray skies above as Floryn lifted her head in wonder. Within a few seconds, the pure, cleansing snow had piled into small mounds at their feet. After a bewildered look from Floryn, they gathered the snow as quickly as they could and returned to the bush.

Upon seeing the piles of snow, the mother and father rabbit exchanged apprehensive looks. They had clearly never seen anything as strange as snow before.

"This snow cleanses and purifies--Please, take it and feed it to your bunnies," Paleo explained gently. Mother and Father Rabbit took deep breaths, carefully scooped up the snow, and fed it to each of the bunnies in turn. All fell silent in anticipation.

After just a few short moments, the pained moans fell silent, and the shaking bunnies were calmed. One by one they opened their eyes and began to slowly hop around. Though they would need some time to recover their full strength, they were alive, and they would recover fully. Everyone sobbed great tears of joy.

After a final thank you from Mother and Father Rabbit, Paleo and Floryn set out together again. Though they had saved the bunnies from their suffering, both of their hearts were still filled with worry. They had both been able to save their people in need, but the safety was only temporary. The elders of the winter were still going to starve, and the children of spring were still going to succumb to disease. Was there any way to save them all?

"The winter needs to thaw...and the spring needs to freeze..." Paleo mumbled to himself.

"Pardon?" said Floryn.

"The winter needs to thaw...and the spring needs to freeze!" he shouted madly, hopping up and down with great joy, but Floryn was still positively perplexed.

"I, Paleo, am the Stag of winter," he explained, unable to contain his excitement. "I carry the season in my heart and soul. I can command the cold and frost of winter, but I never felt the need in the cold regions. Do you not see?" he asked with jubilant glee. "You are Floryn, the Doe of Spring. You are named for the flowers and you have a special connection with them. You carry the warmth of spring in your heart, and you too can command your season! Come with me!"

With all his might, he dashed toward Winter with Floryn chasing behind him. *This is it*, he thought to himself--he must have the answer--this had to be it--

They crossed the threshold of winter, still in a dead sprint. Floryn shivered madly but followed him bravely through lands unknown to her. The snow on the ground was piled so high that it nearly grazed the bottom of her belly as he struggled to get through it.

Finally, Paleo slid through the thick snow to a halt. Out of breath and freezing, Floryn looked around to see snow falling as far in the distance as she could see. Biting winds blew past, and she could feel her bones chilling more by the minute. She had never experienced a cold as deep as this.

"Think about the sun," Paleo whispered in her ear. "Place your front legs together, hold your head up high, close your eyes..." She looked at him, still slightly confused, but closed her eyes. "...Think of the sun. Think of its radiating warmth blowing in gentle breezes that soothe your soul. Think of the sweet melodies of songbirds singing the day away. Think of the flowers, Floryn. Think of the beautiful flowers you were named for and smell their sweet fragrance..."

Suddenly, the fierce chill in the air melted into a summer breeze. The pale gray skies dissolved into clear blue, and the snow on the ground slowly melted away.

Nearby squirrels and chipmunks braved the outside to see the bizarre blue sky, feeling warmth in the air for the first time in their lives. More and more creatures surfaced from the underground, dancing and celebrating the joyful warmth.

The trees grew lush leaves with incredible speed, and grass shot out of the thawed earth. Floryn looked around at the creatures and their bounding joy as they feasted on the now plentiful vegetation. Her heart swelled as she turned to Paleo and smiled. Together, they began to wander aimlessly through the lands, enjoying the happiness and peace that they brought to their people, and to each other.

From that moment forward, the cold and warm regions were married into one, and the whole land shared a single season at a time.

Winter lent the land over to spring when it was time for the food to grow, and the warm summer bowed to the winter when it was time for the frosts to reign. Starvation was a thing of the past, and plagues no longer lingered over the lands. All creatures were eternally grateful to the Doe and Stag for their gift of harmony.

Some elves say that Floryn and Paleo still live, wandering aimlessly through the lands to this day, changing the seasons when the time comes. Others say that they perished long ago, and from the other side of nature they continue their work, moving the seasons through time, forever joined together as one harmonious spirit.

***

Carefully, Gema closed the book and looked at the boys.

"Interesting," said Darion in a tone that was almost sincere.

"That's so cool. So two deer change the seasons every year?" asked Demetri brightly.

"That is what the ancient legends tell us," said Gema. "It's up to us what we believe."

Demetri started to ask how big Paleo's antlers were when a sweet, tantalizing smell wafted through the air from the kitchen. Mom entered the living room with her kind smile finally replacing the exhausted, discouraged grimace from earlier. To the boys' delight, she was carrying four small plates, each with a steaming slice of ruby red berry pie.

"I thought you boys could use a pick me up after such a hard day," she said, handing a slice to Gema as the boys hopped in place, waiting for theirs.

"How did the berries grow so fast?" asked Darion teasingly.

"I gathered them in the woods this morning, goof-ball," she chuckled.

They all sat comfortably, enjoying Mom's delicious pie. Darion laughed out loud as Gema sloppily downed hers almost instantly, and Mom tried to wipe pie filling off of Darion's cheek with her spit, making him turn the same color as the pie. Demetri smiled at the misfortune of his brother, but couldn't help turning his head toward the window. It was pitch black out there now, and he couldn't even see the tree line for the forest. He wondered briefly what would happen if he snuck out one night, just to see what was out there--his sleepy mind drifted toward the story he just heard. Could Floryn and Paleo be out there right now, slowly changing the seasons? He yawned loudly as he recited Gema's words in his mind.

"It's up to us what we believe."

Sorrows and Salamanders

"Mom is going to kill you," Darion said, holding his hand to his mouth to stifle a giggle. Demetri scowled back as he held his hand over a thick piece of Darion's shirt wrapped around his arm, which was dripping blood.

They deliberately walked slowly from the hideout, trying to make the journey home last as long as possible--Demetri felt like his heartbeats were numbered.

Mom loved letting them go outside and have fascinating adventures in the wild forests, but she wasn't as fond of the many injuries that Demetri always seemed to end up with that Darion always seemed to avoid with ease. The last time Demetri had come home with an injury, she told him that drastic measures would be taken if he came home with a single bump or scrape ever again--measures that Demetri tried not to think about. He felt a twinge of sick nervousness fill his stomach more and more with each step closer to the cottage.

"It's--it's not that bad...is it?" he said, slowly pulling the cloth away to peer at his fresh wound.

"Don't do that!" Darion shouted as he smacked Demetri's hand away from the cloth.

"Ugh, why?" Demetri asked, sure to roll his eyes hard enough for Darion to see.

"It's going to start bleeding really badly again," Darion snapped. "Do you want to risk passing out?"

"It's not *that* bad!" Demetri insisted again.

"She's going to have to stitch it," Darion teased as he brushed some of his sandy blond hair out of his blue eyes, chuckling slightly to himself

"No she won't!" Demetri's heart clamored with fear. No injury he had ever gotten was worse than the pain of having a needle shoved into his skin over and over again.

"Oh yeah she will," Darion taunted, dragging his feet dramatically, obviously trying to show Demetri that he was walking unrealistically slow. "It's not going to stop bleeding until she does."

Demetri let out an irritated grunt. "Fine, then can we at least walk just a little slower?"

"Not possible, but why?"

"Because I want to enjoy the little bit of life and freedom I have left."

Darion snickered as he picked up the pace.

As soon as they stepped foot onto the front porch, Mom's kind face appeared in the doorway. Demetri smiled as warmly as he could muster, but his stomach lurched. Her loving smile suddenly morphed as her eyes met his arm, and Demetri was amazed at how quickly she could go from gentle deer to murderous mountain lion.

"Get in the house...now," she whispered.

*Oh God, she's whispering...*Demetri thought to himself. He turned to meet his brother's eyes, but Darion remained as stoic as ever. They shuffled into the house; Demetri's eyes remained fixed on the floor.

"In the kitchen," she whispered again. Mom whispering may have made it seem like Demetri wasn't in for as much trouble as he thought he was, but he knew better. The silence in her whispers was more deadly than the volume of her shouts. He was done for.

Demetri sat silently at the kitchen table, his eyes still fixed on whatever he could find on the floor, or whatever wasn't Mom's eyes. Out of the corner of his eye, he could see Darion's feet over by the doorway trying to tip toe out of the room, trying to escape the wrath of Mom.

"Don't you even think about it, Darion. *Sit.*"

She was still whispering...

Darion grunted, dragged one of the
kitchen chairs into the corner, and sat down
with his arms crossed. Demetri exchanged
a guilty look with his brother, but Darion's
expression remained completely stoic. Mom
left the room, walking briskly with her th
ese-boys-make-me-want-to-rip-my-hair-out
speed and heavy steps.

"She sounds like an earthquake," Darion
chucked softly.

"This isn't funny!" Demetri hissed, but
Darion kept chuckling into his cupped
hands. Demetri, on the other hand, couldn't
have chuckled even if he wanted to. His
heart raced harder and harder as he thought
the same thing to himself over and over
again...*please don't stitch it up, please don't
stitch it up...*

Mom returned with a basin of steaming
water, a bar of homemade soap, and a pile
of white rags. She slammed the basin onto
the table--splashes of hot water went flying
everywhere, but Mom took no notice. She
threw the white rags beside the basin,
slammed the soap onto the table, and threw
herself angrily into the seat facing Demetri.

His heart was pounding furiously in his chest, as if it was trying to interrupt and rapidly explain everything for him, and he desperately wished it could so he didn't have to.

Mom grabbed his arm and pulled off the temporary bandage. Blood started pouring copiously down his arm and began pooling in the floor. She gasped and pressed the bandage back onto his wound. In an attempt to be brave, Demetri took a chance and looked at Mom's face. Her expression was blank, but her cheeks were becoming redder and redder by the minute. Pressure was building...any second now...

"DEMETRI ANBIDIAN! DO YOU HAVE ANY IDEA HOW SERIOUS THIS GASH IS?!"

And there it was.

"I know, Mom..."

"YOU HAD BETTER EXPLAIN YOURSELF RIGHT NOW!"

"I was just trying to wrap a rope around a tree close to the hideout..."

"YOU DON'T GET GASHES LIKE THAT FROM TYING ROPES!"

"I just thought it would be faster if I..." his voice got stuck in his throat.

"IF YOU WHAT?"

"...if I swung to the tree instead of climbing..." he mumbled, feeling his cheeks flush. He braced himself for the rest of her screaming session, but nothing came. When he could finally look up, he saw her staring at him with a look that was somewhere between bewilderment and ferocity.

"JILIAD!" she yelled into the back of the house. Demetri let his gaze fall back to the floor. *Great*, he thought to himself, *she's going to get Dad*. Sure enough, the burly figure of Dad stopped in the doorway of the kitchen, looked at Demetri's arm, and sighed.

"What do you need me to do, Maeryn?"

"I just need one of the curved needles and some thread. Is there still boiling water in the kettle?"

"NO! Mom please! It's not that bad!" he pleaded, shaking uncontrollably.

"It's bad enough to get blood all over my floor!"

Dad left the room as Mom held firmly on Demetri's arm while dipping a white cloth into the basin. With a quick transfer, Demetri felt the old rag lift off of his arm and a scalding one take its place.

"Ow! Mom! That's actually really hot!"

"And you have no one to blame but yourself. Honestly, sometimes I wonder if you have a brain in that hard little skull of yours. You're lucky you can still use your arm. You cut through a little of your muscle." Demetri felt her press harder on his arm, absent-mindedly squeezing hard enough to make the hot water drip out of the rag and onto the floor. "Swinging from the hideout to another tree, what in Akelian were you thinking!?" She pressed harder--Demetri winced.

"I'm guessing you swung from the second floor of your hideout? I can't think of a single good reason to do something so stupid--" she pressed harder, "--be lucky if you survive building that thing--" she pressed harder. Her words became more and more faint through the searing pain shooting through his arm. "--the most careless child I have ever met. Falling into a river because you thought you could jump over it, running into a tree because you wanted to try to run through the forest blindfolded--"

"Mom--" Demetri whispered cautiously.

"Don't you even start Demetri! The next time you think you can...I don't even know how you come up with your crazy ideas... read the stars by standing at the very edge of a cliff while standing on one leg..."

"Mom--" he winced, finding it hard to breathe through the pain.

"And YOU, Darion Anbidian!" She turned away from Demetri to face his brother, who was wearing a stoic expression with his arms crossed.

"Oh here we go," said Darion.

"Don't you roll your eyes at me young man! Why didn't you stop him? Did it ever occur to you to say 'Hey Tree, that may not be such a good idea' or 'Hey, Tree, you're acting like a complete idiot' or even 'Hey Tree, you're going to give Mom another reason to BEAT YOU WITHIN AN INCH OF YOUR LIFE'!?"

Demetri would have shuddered at the last remark, but he couldn't concentrate through the torture his arm was going through.

"I mean, it occurred to me, yeah," Darion admitted with confidence.

"Then why didn't you stop him?!"

"That would be seriously less entertaining for me than watching him swing smack dab into that tree." Darion grinned defiantly from ear to ear. "I mean, WHAM! You should have seen it. Magical moment."

Demetri couldn't see the look Mom was giving to Darion, but he could guess that it was soul shaking. But Darion just gave her an ear to ear grin of satisfaction.

"You," Mom shouted, "are supposed to make sure that this accident seeking, death stalking child keeps his life and limbs, or I will take yours!"

"So no pressure," Darion said with an even voice.

Demetri couldn't help but giggle. Mom's head made a lightning sharp turn and faced Demetri again, and her eyes were full of raging fire. Even his giggle was afraid of her and retreated instantly.

She drew in a deep breath, clearly preparing for a long stammer of loud lecturing, and Demetri cringed and braced himself--

"Here you go, dear," Dad said, appearing in the doorway again with a curved needle in his hand. "You can probably let go of that, by the way," he pointed to Demetri's arm.

"...Right," she conceded as she loosened her grip. Demetri let out a huge sigh of relief, but the relief didn't last long.

"Jil, I need you to hold his arm while I thread the needle."

"Mom PLEASE!!" Demetri begged. "You don't have to stitch it! Really! It doesn't even hurt!" He felt like he was pleading for his life.

"It looks pretty bad, Tree," Dad said as he assessed the gash. Demetri felt his stomach deflate as Dad gently grabbed his arm. Mom turned to Darion.

"I want you out of this room."

In an instant, Darion's expression went from blank to incensed.

"What?! I'm not going anywhere while he's having his arm torn into by a needle!"

"Don't you back talk me young man! You two need to learn how to cope without each other eventually and now seems a good time to start since you didn't have the decency to tell him not to do something so stupid."

Demetri's breath was stolen right out of his chest.

"That's not even fair!" Darion shouted in outrage as he jumped to his feet.

"Life isn't fair."

"He's my brother!"

"He's no more of a brother now than he was when you *didn't* tell him not to swing from that tree!"

"DAD!" Demetri and Darion said together.

"Sorry boys, your mother is right," Dad said sympathetically. Both boys were completely speechless. Demetri couldn't believe it.

"You have chores to do, Darion," Mom said. "Go feed Amphy. Now. And not another word."

The quickest way to anger Darion was to take him away from his brother, no matter what the reason. Demetri looked at Darion as fear welled up in his eyes, and injustice rose in Darion's. His brilliant blue eyes turned to his mother as he defiantly made no motion to leave the room.

Darion stood there for a moment in silence, staring daggers into her. Mom's angry stare was a force to be reckoned with, but Darion had to get it from somewhere. His violent glare made Mom look like a puffed up kitten.

After a coaxing nod from Dad, Darion stormed out of the room, slamming the back door on his way out. Demetri felt like he had been torn in half, and he was finding it hard to breathe.

"Okay, Tree," Dad said, "It's going to be over before you know it."

Mom threaded the needle. Demetri cringed and closed his eyes.

"DAAAAAAAAAD!!"

The blood curdling scream came not from the scared boy with the serious injury, but through the open kitchen window... from outside... from Darion. Demetri opened his eyes and ran for the back door, barely even aware that Mom and Dad were still there, as if they had suddenly faded into the far distance. All that mattered was Darion, and Darion never screamed like that...

He could hear the hurried footsteps of his parents behind him, but he didn't stop. The three of them ran though the clearing until they found Darion just a few feet ahead of them, on his knees, staring at a fuzzy red mass in front of him on the ground--a fuzzy red mass that was not moving.

Demetri froze, somehow unsure of what he was seeing yet completely aware, and unaware of his freely bleeding arm. Dad walked right past Demetri to Darion. Demetri watched Dad look down at the unmoving mass, let out a deep sigh, and gently place his arm on his son's shoulder.

"Fix him, Dad," Darion's voice was thick with tears. "He's sick! Help him!"

"Son--"

"You can fix anything! Fix him!"

"I can't fix this--"

"Mom!" Darion looked up at Mom, who still stood beside Demetri with tears in her eyes.

"He's sick!" Darion called out to her. "Get him some water or a blanket! Get him something, anything! Help me Mom!"

But Mom remained still, her eyes full of empathy. She didn't speak a word, but Demetri understood. His voice seemed to have left him as well. He couldn't breathe. He couldn't think. He knew what this was, and he knew his brother needed him. But he couldn't move. His feet, his stupid feet that could run through forests at deer speed, couldn't even carry him a few feet to his brother. His knees were going weak, whether from the loss of blood still pouring down his arm or the shock of what was in front of him, he couldn't tell.

"Son," Dad whispered. "He's gone. There's nothing I can--"

"NO! He's not gone!" Darion desperately pleaded, his voice weak and shaking. "He can't be gone! Why won't you help him?! Why won't you help me?!"

Dad looked up at Mom, and she nodded as tears finally spilled over onto her face. Demetri felt a hot, wet prickling in his eyes and a heavy lump in his throat...yet he still couldn't move. Why couldn't he move?

Mom walked forward and knelt beside Darion, leaving Demetri all alone. She wrapped her loving arms around him, and Demetri just looked on helplessly as his brother, the strongest kid in the world, sobbed uncontrollably into his mother's shoulder. He couldn't hold back anymore--he didn't even want to try--and the tears flowed down his face...he hoped Darion wouldn't look up and see...he just wanted to be strong for him...

The sun was setting in the clear sky, and everything was turning orange. The air was warm and the sky was beautiful...but Demetri had never felt so cold, and the world never looked so dark and ugly.

Dad reached down and gently lifted Amphy off of the ground. "I have to bury him, son."

"You can't!" Darion shouted through heavy sobs. "He'll suffocate! He'll get lonely without me..."

His voice trailed off.

"...He'll be lonely without me..."

"Please my son," Mom whispered gently. "Just tell him you love him. Tell him goodbye."

Demetri looked on as Darion leaned away from his mother, just long enough to wrap his arms around Amphy for the last time. Dad stood slowly, gingerly carrying the youngest member of the Anbidian family in his arms, and he turned toward Demetri. He knew Dad was walking toward him...he knew what was coming...

He wanted to turn and run, never to say goodbye, but his stupid knees were weak and his feet wouldn't move.

It seemed to happen out of nowhere, and Demetri couldn't remember seeing it, but somehow Dad was right in front of him. Demetri looked down and saw Amphy--eyes closed with no breath--and he found that he couldn't breathe either. He did his best to steady himself, heaving deep, focused breaths as reached his out his hand to touch his fox--*his* fox--it wasn't until this moment that Demetri realized...Amphy really was his fox too...and he realized it all too late.

His little fox's body was so cold, so still, so lifeless.

He knew that this was his last chance to tell Amphy that he loved him, to tell him how much fun it was to race him through the woods, to throw sticks to him in the meadow, to sleep with his warm body beside him in the grass. He opened his mouth to speak, but couldn't find the words. He tried again, but nothing would leave his throat.

His blood went cold, and his tears flowed hot. All he could do was hold his head to Amphy's and wrap his good arm around his soft neck. Then, before he knew it, Dad was walking away... and Amphy was gone.

Mom helped Darion to his feet, and they shuffled mournfully toward Demetri, her arm still around Darion's shaking body. As they reached him, she put her other arm around his shoulder. Still in shock with his head swimming, Demetri turned toward the house as well.

Gema stood in the doorway, her long hair flowing freely in the gentle winds, and her face reflecting the pain Demetri felt in his chest.

"Oh, my boys," she whispered as they approached the door. "My poor boys..."

A deep, solemn silence hung over the family, following them into the house and staying while Demetri's arm was stitched up by Mom, but this time, Darion was allowed to be by his side.

It followed the boys out to the front porch with Gema, and for the first time, Darion sat down on his wooden stool without a single word of protest. The three of them sat in silence for a moment with Demetri glancing over to his brother every few seconds, but Darion was staring unseeingly into the forest behind Gema. The silence was so deep and heavy that Gema's whisper felt like a piercing roar.

"I know how you feel," she whispered gently.

Demetri looked at her through misty eyes, but couldn't find his voice to reply. He glanced over at his brother again, but Darion's empty eyes still stared at nothing.

"You can feel a burning in your chest," she went on, no longer whispering, "an ache that feels like both fire and ice, an ache that you can't shed. You feel confused and betrayed by the world at the same time, because the world doesn't feel any different. But how can the world not feel any different? The world has lost something so special and so wonderful...it *should* feel different...but it doesn't...and it just doesn't make any sense." She let out a mournful sigh. "You know in your mind that he's gone, and that he can't come back. But you still feel him. You still look toward the woods expecting to see him trotting up to the front porch, smiling and wagging his bushy tail, hoping you had roast deer for dinner and saved him some scraps. You know he's gone, so why does it feel like he'll be back any minute now? You feel like the world hasn't missed a beat, even though your heart feels like it will never beat right again. You think it's not fair, and you've been cheated by the world."

"It's *not* fair," Demetri whispered breathlessly.

"I know, my dear. I know," she said lovingly. "Wounds of the heart bring far more pain than wounds of the flesh. But take heart, my grandsons. The wounds in

your hearts are fresh. They sting sharply
and bleed freely right now. But just like
that horrible wound on your arm, Tree,
your heart will heal in time." She gently
took Demetri's hand into hers and smiled
a watery, empathetic smile. Demetri felt
like he would never smile again, and spoke
through his shaking voice and simpering
face.

"I just want to see him again...I'll never
see him again. I miss him so much."

"And you'll always miss him, but one day,
it won't hurt so much anymore. One day
you'll look back on the memory of Amphy
and smile, thinking of how much happiness
he brought you." She gently squeezed his
hand.

"But why?" Darion said abruptly. His
voice was so sharp that both Gema and
Demetri jumped slightly. After gently letting
go of Demetri's hand, Gema leaned back in
her chair and focused her eyes on Darion.

"What do you mean, dear?"

"Why did this have to happen? He wasn't
hurting anything." Darion spoke quickly
and frantically, as if he were trying to get

a whole thought out before succumbing to more tears. "He was just a fox! It's not like Amphy being alive hurt anyone, but now he's not here and everyone is hurt. It doesn't make any sense. He shouldn't have had to... to..." his voice broke, trailing off into soft sobs.

"Darion," she said gently, "Death is a very painful and difficult thing to handle, but it is something that has to happen."

"But *why?* There's no reason for it. None. It's a stupid thing and it doesn't need to happen."

In the tense silence that followed these words, Demetri couldn't seem to get them out of his mind. *He's right*, he thought to himself. After all, the world wasn't a better place because people or animals or even plants died. So how could something so dark and horrible need to happen in this world? Death should be something that people tried to stop, because it's not natural. It can't be.

Slowly and gingerly, Gema reached under her green blanket and pulled out the book. Demetri found that he felt no sense of excitement, no ecstatic happiness, no burning curiosity...nothing. His insides were numb and empty.

"We need to continue this in the house--we don't have much more daylight--but I think there is a story that you two need to hear, if you will let me tell it."

Unable to force any enthusiasm, Demetri said nothing as Gema rose from her rocking chair, headed toward the front door. Both of them solemnly followed. Darion slumped over on the couch with his eyes fixed on the floor and, for the first time, offered no groans or protests.

"This story comes from Rhodarion, the Red Kingdom. It's an ancient tale about a creature that felt the very same way that you two feel about death right now."

With great care, she opened the book and flipped to the right page.

***

In the lush forests under the southern mountains, a giant, fiery red salamander proudly roamed the lands. With a body as large as a lion and an ego as large as the world, he held his head high as he prowled through the forest. He was the only creature of his kind, and he preferred it that way. Not just anyone could handle his immense power, in his not-so-humble opinion. Though he was pompous and incredibly self centered, in his mind he had every right to be. This special salamander could create red hot fire with just the touch of his slimy paws, a dangerous power that he was not afraid to show off.

The salamander, called Oraibis, was so smug that none of the forest creatures could stand to be around him for very long. Oraibis had only one friend, an unusually small brown bear named Pylen. Though he was still just as smug and pompous with Pylen as he was with every other creature, Pylen had much more patience and could tolerate his self centered nature. Pylen was simply happy to have someone to call a friend. Just like Oraibis, Pylen had a difficult time making friends, owing to his unusually small size.

One fateful day, the forest air was thick with fog as a heavy rain swept through the hot air. Oraibis and Pylen wrestled around in a mud puddle, enjoying the refreshing cool rain as they gleefully flung mud at each other. They slipped and slid and pranced and played for hours and hours, even as the skies grew darker and the rain pounded harder. Despite the gloomy weather, they were both as gleeful as a sunny meadow.

Exhausted from their muddy merriment, they rested their mud soaked bodies under a nearby tree. Oraibis gazed peacefully into the distance and noticed a small, sodden bush. A smug smirk stretched out on his slimy red face, and he turned to his friend.

"Pylen, I can easily throw a fireball and set that bush ablaze. Would you like to see?"

Pylen looked toward the bush and let out a small sigh. "My dear friend, you are a powerful creature. Yet you have met your match. Water is greater than fire, and you shall not set that bush ablaze."

Oraibis felt a surge of hot anger and could feel the burning of a new challenge. Without a word, he formed a white hot fireball in his sticky paws, rising from his muddy seat as fast as he could...too fast...

His feet slipped in the slippery mud--his body was out of control--and the fireball blazed through air as his head crashed back onto the ground.

Violent screams were all he could hear; his blood ran cold.

He looked up to his friend as quickly as he could, but froze in fear at the sight before his eyes. Pylen had been caught by the fire... and his entire head was alight with bright flames.

His screams pierced into Oraibis' soul. Terrified and flushed with guilt, Oraibis knew that Pylen would not survive...he had brought death upon his only friend.

Oraibis turned away and did the only thing he could do: he ran. Slipping and sliding on the muddy forest floor, he scrambled and staggered as far away as he possibly could, until he could find no more breath and no more strength.

After many woeful hours, he found a small cave just big enough for him, crawled inside, and wept. His pride dissolved into shame, and his confidence fizzled into guilt. He closed his eyes tight, desperately trying to erase the image of his dear friend, screaming and burning...his face melting and cracking... all because of his deranged showing off.

I will never use my flames again, he thought to himself as he fell into an uneasy sleep. *No matter what may come, never again will I curse this land with fire.*

***

"Gema," Demetri interjected, "I mean no disrespect, but this story isn't exactly making me feel any better. The last thing I want to hear about is something else dying." He turned to Darion, who was still staring at the floor. Demetri could see wet marks on the thighs of his pants from his falling tears.

"I can stop now, if you want," said Gema as she closed the book, looking somewhat disappointed. "But if you will be patient, I can assure you that this story holds comfort for you...if you'll allow me to continue."

Demetri looked at his Grandmother, whose mischievous twinkle was gone, a melancholic but comforting expression taking its place. He nodded his head in approval, but Darion made no move at all. Not knowing why he did it, Demetri scooted as close to Darion as he possibly could. Maybe he wanted to comfort his brother, maybe he just needed Darion closer to comfort himself. Without even realizing what he was doing, he put his hand arm around his brother's shoulders...but Darion's eyes remained fixed on the floor.

Gema opened the book, searching with her eyes to find where she left off.

***

Many years had passed before Oraibis emerged out of the cave that he now called his home. He stretched widely and gazed toward the sky, painted with the pale lavender light of an early sunrise, the inky black of night barely clinging to the corners of the horizon. As he stared into the beauty of the eternal sky, his ever deepening sadness enveloped him once again.

A deer frolicked through the nearby trees, and Oraibis crept back into his cave.

He could never allow himself to be near
another living creature ever again, for their
own safety. He was a monster, and monsters
could not have friends. Monsters hurt their
friends...and killed them in the end.

He began to wonder why he bothered
leaving his cave, why he even bothered to
wake up in the morning. Every day he awoke
to nothing but the pain of his isolation. He
could wander the forest, but he had no one
with him to enjoy its beauty. He could go
to his watering hole and enjoy a refreshing
drink, but there would be no one to share it
with. So what was the point of leaving? His
only comfort was knowing that, while he
may be painfully lonely, the rest of the world
was safe from his flame.

The simple joy of even a bland
conversation, just the ability to use his
voice, was nothing but a distant memory to
him. Not a single moment passed where he
could not think of Pylen...Pylen would smile
and laugh with him. He would have raced
him through the forest until they were both
exhausted and breathless. He would have
sat beside him and just talked randomly

about everything and nothing at the same time. He would have--but he couldn't. He was long gone, his voice just a faint memory with nothing to rekindle it, and it was all his, Oraibis', fault...

Oraibis shook his head violently, trying to shake himself from his thoughts. As he looked through the mouth of his cave, the faint trails among the trees seemed to be calling his name, and the urge to wander was impossible to ignore. Not knowing why he was doing it, he slowly left the home that was his prison, wandering slowly and aimlessly through the early morning forest.

The lush grass felt cool and wet from the early morning dew as he meandered through the trees with his head hung low, but suddenly, he felt the sting of what felt like splinters beneath his feet. After looking at the ground beneath his feet, he gasped with horror.

Parched, sickly yellow grass stretched across the land where lush, emerald grass once grew. Dead, petrified trees stood like skeletons in a graveyard, and the putrid smell of rotting decay oozed into Oraibis' nostrils. The stench was so potent that he could barely breathe--the only living animals he could see were fleeing as fast as they could--no cheerful bird songs or scurrying squirrel steps fell upon his ears--the air was as silent and still as death.

"The forest is ill," said a soft-spoken voice from somewhere behind him. Oraibis twitched slightly in his skin, but kept his eyes on the ill-fated forest. Whoever this creature was, he would be safer with Oraibis' back to him.

"Yes," said Oraibis, "but it will recover."

"You lie to yourself, a shameful act," said the voice in a surprisingly peaceful tone. "This illness will surely spread and take many lives. You can sense it."

"I sense nothing," Oraibis replied defiantly, snorting.

"You sense it and you lie. You are the only creature of your kind, and you can feel the weak, frail thread of life still tethered to this forest."

"Why are you talking to me?" Oraibis burst out angrily, turning sharply to face this stranger. Behind him stood a bear--a

bear with scars around his head--a bear
that was unusually smaller than most other
bears--

"P-Pylen?" Oraibis could barely find his
breath as the bear beamed back at him.

"But you...you were..." Oraibis stuttered,
unable to find words.

"Water is greater than fire, remember?"
Pylen smiled wisely at his dear friend. "I
simply rolled in the mud to smother the
flames. By the time I looked up, you were
gone. I have been searching for you for many
long years."

"I thought I--I thought you--" Tears
were welling in Oraibis' eyes as he wished
desperately for forgiveness, but Pylen merely
gave a gently smile.

"We will have plenty of time later. For
now, the forest needs your gift."

Oraibis turned to gaze at the wilting
woodland before him. "There is nothing I can
do to save this part of the forest."

"Of course not," Pylen said peacefully,
staring the forest ahead of him. "But there is
something you can do to save the rest of the
forest."

Oraibis turned to Pylen, anger bubbling in his gut, but Pylen did not return his stare.

"No," he said forcefully.

"If you use your flame..."

"No."

"Dear friend, be reasonable..."

"NO!" screamed Oraibis, feeling fiery anger surge through his body. "You would have me condemn this forest to death!"

"It is already condemned," said Pylen, his voice still calm and wise, his eyes still focused on the forest.

"Not by me. It will not be me!"

"It has to be you," Pylen countered, his fur-less face still not looking into the eyes of his friend. Oraibis wished Pylen would get angry with him, to give him justification for his own white-hot anger. He wanted Pylen to look at him, but he wouldn't. Was the small bear ashamed of him? Why wouldn't he look at him? He could feel guilt building underneath his anger.

Silence fell between the two friends; Oraibis could think of nothing to say. He just wished that he, Pylen, would understand.

After a few long, tense moments, Pylen finally spoke.

"You run from death, and you hide from it, cursing its name. But you curse and fear what you don't understand. Everything has its time, Oraibis. Everything and everyone will die. You cannot flee from it, you cannot predict it, and you cannot stop it. It needs to happen. This parasitic illness will continue to spread through all forests, leaving the land stagnant and unable to sustain any life at all. It is *this* forest's time. It cannot continue to exist like this, hovering somewhere between life and death. If it does not die, all will suffer this fate." Pylen finally turned to stare deeply into Oraibis' eyes.

"Don't you see, Oraibis? New life cannot start without death. Without death, there can be no life."

Oraibis looked toward the falling forest.

"You cannot ask this of me. I cannot be death. I am not a murderer."

"No," whispered Pylen gently. "You hold the key to allowing new life to emerge from the dust of the dead. You are a hero, Oraibis, not a murderer."

Pylen's words were full of a great intelligence that Oraibis had never heard before. Even though Oraibis' task would break his heart, how could he ignore such wisdom?

Feeling the icy grip of fear around his long throat, Oraibis drew a deep breath. As his anger turned into determination and his fear to purpose, he strode sorrowfully into the center of the ill fated woods. His paws grew hotter by the moment. Closing his eyes tight, he braced himself. Within seconds, the parched grass was ablaze--the still silence was replaced with the deafening roar of violent flames--the fire spread rapidly to the surrounding grass and trees, yet Oraibis stood his ground, feeling the radiating heat bouncing off of his slimy body. There he stood, a sentinel in the flames, with tears streaking down his face and falling into the hot earth beneath him. He had done it. He killed the forest.

The flames began to flicker and die. Eerie black smoke lingered; the hot ash glowed red. Yet still Oraibis stood; still he wept.

After what seemed like a lifetime to poor Oraibis, the smoke began to float away. He trudged through the graveyard of ash with guilt rising in his chest and overflowing into tears, dripping onto the charred land. Gazing through the veil of tears, Oraibis could just make out the silhouette of Pylen in the distance. Slowly, he staggered toward the comfort of his only friend.

He stood with his back to the desolation, facing Pylen but unable to look at him, unable to even speak. Thoughts of the forest flooded into his mind. How beautiful it must have been before the sickness took root. Lush, beautiful trees dancing in the breeze... deer grazing on the soft grass...all gone, without a chance of return.

"My dear friend, do not weep, for you have yet to see the wonder of your gift," said Pylen gently.

"There is no wonder in death," Oraibis whispered, shaking.

"Just take one last look at what you have done."

Reluctantly, Oraibis turned his head to the ashen patch of earth, ready to take in the horror of what he had done--but what he saw was far from what he had expected to see.

Tiny green spouts were emerging from the ashes, stretching for the sun, merrily twinkling with dewdrops on their leaves. The sprouts, Oraibis noticed, seemed to grow all in a line...the same line that he walked to leave the ashes, leaving a trail of tears behind him...

He looked to Pylen, whose face was full of joy and wisdom, and a great grin spread on Oraibis' face. He raced through the ashes, sprinkling tears in every corner that he could--but this time, they were tears of joy.

After many happy tears had soaked into the ash, Oraibis trotted back to Pylen, finally free from grudge he held against his gift. Never again did he have to feel the pain of imprisonment or isolation, and never again did he call himself a monster. After all, monsters don't have friends, and Oraibis had Pylen.

The two friends raced through the forest and wallowed in mud puddles to their hearts content for many ages. For exactly how long, no one knows for sure. But one thing was absolutely certain: whenever life was ready to meet its end, Oraibis was always there to guide the dying, to be a friend to those returning to the great Spirit of Nature, with Pylen always by his side.

***

Gema tenderly closed the book and looked at Darion, who looked up from the floor for the first time.

"Come here, Darion," she held out her hand for him, and he slowly stood up, walked over to her chair, and took her hand. A fire crackled in the living room fireplace, and the flickering light showed the sorrow on Darion's face.

"Sit with me," she said, patting her lap. It was a clear sign of his grief that he didn't refuse. He sat down without so much as a whimper of protest.

"Do you understand, Grandson?" She whispered as she gently placed her hand on his cheek.

"....I'm not sure," he mumbled, his voice breaking.

"I know it's hard to understand, but everything has to die. Birds, squirrels, trees, Amphy...even you and me. If there were no death before you and I were put on this earth, you and I wouldn't even exist. The life cycle is intricate and terribly confusing, but without death and decay, new life can't emerge..."

Darion tried to lower his head in despair, but she gently lifted it with her hand still on his cheek, and looked him in the eye. Demetri saw a tear trickle down his heartbroken face.

"Amphy's death is tragic, and he died leaving a hole in all of our hearts..." she continued gently, "...but life will continue. His death, and all death, makes life itself possible. And you cannot ask for a purpose more noble than that. Amphy gave the earth a gift when he laid his body to rest, as will you and I when we die."

Darion sniffed. "Will we see him again? You know... when we die?"

Gema leaned back into her rocking chair and looked out the living room window, where the tree line was barely visible through the deep blanket of night. Darion rose from her lap and sat beside Demetri on the couch once again.

"What happens to the spirits of the dead is not fully understood," she finally said, not looking away from the window. "Do we pass on into some other world? Or do our spirits return to the mystical spirit of our great earth? That is a question that even this book does not have the answer to--and nor do I. But I can tell you this: our spirits have to go somewhere when our time on earth is done, and they will wander for all of eternity, wherever it is that they go. Eternity is an unfathomably long amount of time. So, chances are, you will see Amphy again sometime during your eternal wanderings."

Darion gave a weak smile, and Gema smiled in return. Unable to control himself, Demetri hugged Darion as tightly as he could, tears positively streaming down his face.

"Ach...get off of me. You trying to break my ribs?"

"I'm just so happy to see you *smile!*" Demetri squealed, still not letting go.

"Oh come on, you big baby," Darion said with another faint smile as he nudged himself free of his brother. "We should go help mom with dinner."

"With my arm sliced in half?!" Demetri said in false shock, trying to sound cheery.

Darion gave a weak chuckle, clearly trying to hide the sadness on his face.

"I dare you to try to give her that excuse."

"Ha ha...no thanks," Demetri said as he stood up, stretched, and kissed Gema on the cheek before disappearing through the kitchen door. Darion paused in the doorway and turned to look at Gema.

"Thanks," he said simply, and she simply smiled in return.

A few days later, Demetri and Darion were up with the sun, ready to start another day of building the hideout.

"Um, Tree?" Darion mumbled as they were getting dressed in their room.

"Yeah?" Demetri said, stifling a yawn and digging for a shirt in his wooden chest.

"Before we head out to the hideout, d'you think we could stop and see Amphy?"

Demetri looked at Darion, surprised. Darion had been avoiding the backyard ever since Dad had buried him...

"Uh, sure--If you want."

Once the boys were dressed and had eaten their fill of breakfast, they walked out the back door, through the yard, and came to a halt at a small round stone etched with a few words in Dad's handwriting.

Amphor Anbidian
Beloved friend and brother

To their delight, green sprouts were already growing out of the dirt right above where Amphy's body now rested. They looked at each other and couldn't speak, but understood each other's silence. They both smiled before departing, headed toward the hideout and the next great adventure, laughing and exchanging fond memories of their favorite fox.

The Day and The Night

The summer may have been coming
to an end, but that didn't stop the sun
from radiating relentless heat, as the boys
discovered a few days later. Sweating and
panting, they finally arrived at their hideout
clearing after a long hour's worth of hiking
through the sticky heat.

"Well," huffed Demetri, flopping down
on the soft grass, "At least we don't get lost
anymore."

"That's because dad made a trail, Tree,"
barked Darion. "Any idiot can follow a trail."

Demetri just stuck his tongue out at him. "It's not a super-obvious trail," he mumbled in defense as Darion staggered to the little pond.

If there's anything that makes Darion even more of a sour berry, it's the heat, Demetri thought to himself as he watched Darion splash water on his arms and face. Hopefully, something would come in to relive the heat soon, some cloud cover, rain, anything. Darion wasn't going to be in the mood to get too much work done with the fort if the heat didn't let up.

"So," Demetri shouted over to Darion, "What do we need to get done today?"

Darion sulked over to Demetri and sat down beside him.

"Well, if you can keep from killing yourself--" he shot a disbelieving look at him "--we need to finish the top floor of the tree fort. We need more wood for the floor and we need to start figuring out what to do for a balcony."

"We also need a ladder of some sort," Demetri added. "I hate having to throw that stupid rope up to the branch and climb it."

"I'm surprised you haven't broken your arm yet," said Darion, but Demetri just ignored him.

"We also need to think about a way to make a ladder that only we can use, you know what I mean? It's not much of a fort if anyone can get to it."

Darion nodded his head in agreement, staring at the clear pond, thinking. "You said something about a rope ladder yesterday," he pondered out loud. "How would you feel about making a good strong one out of nothing but rope? No wood at all. We could build a small tunnel on the tree for it to fit into, and disguise the tunnel with bark from trees. When we're done, the tunnel will just disappear and look like it's a part of the tree."

"Oh wow, that is brilliant!" Demetri beamed. "Where did you come up with that?"

"I was thinking about it last night," said Darion, looking away from Demetri. "I... couldn't sleep."

Demetri didn't say a word, but he understood. Memories and thoughts of Amphy had been plaguing his nights as well.

He knew there were no words to comfort his brother, so he just placed his consoling hand on Darion's shoulder.

"So," said Darion, obviously trying to change the subject, "would you rather work on the ladder or the floor and rails for the second story?"

Demetri groaned. "I think not having floors is the bigger of the two problems," he said with defeat in his voice. He hated climbing the rope to get up there and would much rather work on that, but he knew he was much more likely to hurt himself on the missing floor than the climbing rope.

"Let's get to it then," Darion said as he stood up, extending his hand for Demetri to grab. "And for the love of Akelian, don't break your arm."

After the arduous climb up the rope, the two boys set to work, using the nails Dad had given them and a pile of flat wood to hammer out a decent floor. Within only a few short moments, both boys were sweating profusely.

"I could make my own river with my sweat!" Darion called out from the other side of the floor, obviously extremely perturbed.

Demetri shouted back to him, "We should go for a dip in the pond when we're--AAAHHHH! OH HEL--HELP!"

Demetri shrieked like a little girl and scrambled to get away, but he fell right through one of the holes in the floor--plummeting hard and fast, hitting the ground with a loud thud.

"Demetri!" Darion shouted, hopping over the holes in the floor to get a good look at him. "Are you okay?"

"Get that thing away!"

"Tree are you hurt?"

"No! Just GET THAT THING AWAY!" he shrieked, panicking. Darion looked around to find the culprit of Demetri's fears. A simple green and blue lizard just a little bigger than his hand was resting in a patch of sunlight. He sighed, chuckling to himself as he shook his head.

"...and I may have hurt my ankle..." Demetri mumbled, but Darion heard him.

"I asked you to do one simple thing," Darion shouted down to him, failing to mask his annoyance. "Just one simple little thing. Don't hurt yourself. All over a little--"

"Just get rid of it! Kill it!" Demetri screamed, but Darion just looked at him.

"I am not going to kill this poor thing just because you have a stupid fear of lizards."

"Please, Dare, please just kill it," Demetri whispered frantically, shaking.

Darion just sighed. Without any fear or hesitation, he gently picked up the lizard and held him with one hand. The little guy gave no protest at all as Darion slid carefully down the rope.

"No! Get it AWAY!" Demetri squealed as he limped away from his brother, but Darion just ignored him and walked a short way into the woods, setting the little guy down on a fallen tree log right in another patch of sun.

He returned to find Demetri sitting by the pond, rubbing a badly swollen ankle. Darion took off his shirt yet again, dunked it into the cool pond water, wrung it out, and wrapped it around Demetri's ankle.

"At this rate, I'll have no more shirts by next week," Darion said jokingly, even though it was absolutely true. Demetri just scowled in silence.

"Pretty stupid, bro," Darion teased, but Demetri was in no mood to listen to his brother's taunts. He was hot, sticky, had just been scared to death, and now his ankle was throbbing and swelling more by the minute. They hadn't even gotten started on the tree fort.

Demetri tried not to look at Darion as he watched him disappear into the woods again, not knowing or caring why he had wandered off. How was he, Demetri, supposed to work on the floor now? He thought vaguely of trying to get up there anyway to see if he could manage, but after trying to put weight on his ankle for a measly second, he realized that it was going to be impossible. *There goes another day of working on the hideout*, he thought bitterly to himself.

"Here," said Darion from behind him. Demetri turned to see him holding a stick that he had fashioned into a crutch. "We're going to have to go home. Mom is going to want to look at that ankle."

There was no mocking or ridicule in his brother's voice, and Demetri wondered fleetingly if Darion was having a rare moment of sympathy. He looked into Darion's eyes and saw the same deep sadness he was always fighting back these days. He certainly hadn't been the same since Amphy's death, and it wasn't like him at all to miss out on a chance to pick on his brother. Feeling sympathetic himself, Demetri smiled at Darion and gratefully took the primitive crutch.

"Well, look on the bright side," said Demetri, "At least I didn't break my arm."

Darion chuckled.

Back at the cottage, Mom was thankfully preoccupied with harvesting vegetables out of the back garden. With her blissfully ignorant of Demetri's injury for the moment, Dad sat him down on the living room couch to take a good look at it. Carefully, he turned his ankle from side to side, examining it closely as Demetri tried to hide a wince.

"It's just a mild strain," he finally said to Demetri's relief.

"So I didn't break it? I can still work on the hideout?" he asked hopefully.

"I would give it at least a week before going on an hour long hike to get to that clearing," Dad said wisely as he propped Demetri's leg up with a couple of soft pillows. "Just keep it elevated for a little bit and you'll be just fine. I have to go hunting now, so if you need anything, holler for Gema or your mother. Will you be okay?"

Demetri just snorted and folded his arms. He heard Dad chuckle slightly to himself before stepping out of the room, but that didn't make him feel any more light hearted about the situation. Darion pulled up the rocking chair and sat beside him.

"Look on the bright side," he said as he rocked harder than was necessary, "It probably won't be as hot out in a week."

At that moment, Gema shuffled through the living room door carrying a freshly baked roll in one hand and an apple in the other.

"Goodness me!" she exclaimed with her crackly voice as she caught sight of Demetri. "What happened here?"

Demetri's face turned sour and he looked away, arms still crossed.

"He got scared by a lizard and fell out of the hideout," said Darion, clearly trying not to laugh.

"It's not funny!" Demetri argued. "It was a million degrees out there so why in Akelian was that stupid thing just sitting out in the sun? Was it trying to roast itself for the birds?"

"It's probably cold underground," Darion said thoughtfully as he stood up, relinquishing his chair to Gema. She carefully lowered herself into it and munched sloppily on her apple. They all sat in silence for a moment as Gema chewed and Demetri sulked.

"Why did it scare you?" Gema finally asked when her apple was nothing more than a core. Demetri didn't answer, but Darion couldn't stop himself any longer--howling laughter burst out of his mouth.

"He's terrified of lizards," he said between chortles, wiping tears out of the corners of his eyes.

"You would be too if your brother told you that their bites made your eyeballs dissolve and then you *die*," Demetri hissed, but Darion just laughed harder.

"I was three! What do you expect?!" Demetri shouted defiantly.

"Now Tree, you know that's not true, right?" Gema asked gently while ripping her roll in half. Darion shook with laughter.

"Of course I know now, but I was three!" he repeated. "Every time I see one, I don't know I just panic. Darion was supposed to kill it but *no,* he had to go and drop that thing off in the woods. Now it might come back!"

Gema gasped. "Demetri Anbidian, I am surprised at you. For someone who loves the elves and their culture so much, you should know better than to kill an innocent creature."

"I don't like them," he mumbled, arms still crossed.

"Regardless," she said in an uncharacteristically serious tone, "you are supposed to be equal to the animals, not place yourself above them. Why do you have the right to decide that the lizard has to die?

If he didn't like you, would he be allowed to kill you?"

Darion stopped laughing. She never raised her voice, nor did she need to. Gema never got angry with the two of them, but even her calm disappointment felt all wrong, like misplaced notes in a familiar song. She rocked back and forth in her chair, chewing her roll contently while the three of them sat in awkward silence. Demetri looked over to see Darion staring out the window, but looking at nothing. Suddenly, Gema stood carefully, without saying a word, and shuffled out of the room. Demetri had nothing to say to his brother, so he sat there in silence, letting him stare out of the window with melancholy in his eyes.

"Demetri," Gema's voice called out from the doorway into the hall. "I have a story that I think you should hear. Would you care to join me on the front porch?"

Despite his throbbing ankle and sour mood, he couldn't help but smile. *At least the day won't be a total waste,* he thought to himself as he grabbed his makeshift crutch, wincing slightly as he rose. He was relieved to see a delighted smile on her face as he hobbled toward the front door. She turned to Darion.

"Would you care to join us?"

Darion turned to face them but seemed to be in a slight daze, as if they had interrupted a deep thought.

"Yeah, actually. Sounds good."

Demetri gaped at him, positively bewildered. Darion stood up and smiled gleefully, as if nothing in Akelian would bring him more joy than to listen to the stories he had always despised.

"You feeling okay there, bro?" Demetri asked, slightly worried.

"Yeah, definitely," he said, turning to look at Gema. "It's nice to escape to another world sometimes."

She gave an understanding nod and smiled.

Thankfully, gray storm clouds blew in with wet winds and the promise of rain, making the heat just the least bit more bearable.

"Now then," said Gema as she took up her place in the rocking chair, thumbing through the book. "We have reached a very interesting part in this book. The time of the ancient creatures is over, you see. They've all done their job, making Akelian a land of peace and paradise, full of the many plants and animals we see all around us. Now, we say goodbye to the time of the ancient creatures, and say hello to the first elves in recorded history."

"Really? Wow!" Demetri beamed with excitement.

"Oh yes," Gema said with a chuckle. "Some say that they sprang from the life-giving waters of the river--others say that they were birthed from a hole in a tree--others even believe that they emerged directly from the earth itself. But however they came into being, the first two elves finally walked the lands."

"Two?" asked Darion.

"Oh, yes. You see, they were twins," she explained with a thoughtful look. Demetri and Darion exchanged looks of warm excitement.

"Another set of twins!" Gema said. "And just like the two of you, they couldn't be more different from each other."

Her gaze fell to the pages in her lap.

***

The pale light of morning hung low in the sky, and the inky blue of night conceding to the slowly rising sun. A crisp breeze swept through endless fields of tall grass, where two brand new beings clung to slumber, holding each other contently. Long strands of black and white hair flowed everywhere, enveloping them in a swirl of silky warmth. Though the morning sun was unyielding, they were unwilling to wake, and unwilling to let each other go.

Birds chirped merry songs all around them, coaxing them gently into wakefulness. They stretched, yawned, and finally let go of each other. Two twin girls stood side by side in the early morning light--the first elves of the world.

They were the most lovely creatures to ever grace Akelian with their presence, yet they were as different from each other as night and day. One sister, Deyja, looked up to the rising sun and shuddered, thinking longingly of the deep night from which they were just aroused. To Deyja, the color of her raven hair was the only color fit for the sky, glowing with the light of the moon, as pale as her ivory skin. Her cold, gray eyes seemed to detest the sting of the bright sun, and she wanted to disappear into the shadows of the forest.

Creya, on the other hand, looked to the beaming sun and smiled. She could stay in the fields under the brilliant light forever, feeling its radiating warmth on her platinum blond hair, smiling at the friendly creatures of the land with her sweet eyes of vibrant turquoise.

The sisters were as different as night and day in every way, but they loved each other dearly. Knowing that Creya would not be happy lurking in the shadows, and Deyja would not be happy under the radiating sun, the two elves separated with the promise to find each other again soon under the pale dusk sky, the perfect marriage of night and day.

Deyja journeyed for the deepest forests in the highest mountains, full of caves and shadows. Through her travels, she connected more and more with the spirit of the night, with its deep mysteries and dark secrets. The bats and wolves that roamed the forest after sunset became her dearest friends, walking alongside her in the pale moonlight. With caves and shadows to shield her and friends to walk by her side, Deyja saw no reason to face the light. She spent less and less time in the face of day, and eventually, she looked up to the sun for the last time.

After many, many years surrounded in darkness with few for company, the darkness began to invade her mind as well. Though she was meant to exist in harmony with nature, she began to see herself as a superior being, the most important being in all of Akelian. She was, after all, the most beautiful creature in all the world. Why should the common creatures not respect and serve her?

By the light of the full moon on a shimmering night, she wandered over to a small pond and gazed at the beautiful reflection of her smug smirk. As she brushed her silky hair, still staring at her own radiant beauty, she thought about the rest of the creatures in the forest.

They should be grateful to be in the presence as one so beautiful as I, she thought to herself as she slowly ran her fingers through her hair. *They should worship me and be overjoyed to do my bidding.*

Over time, she grew ever more cold and cruel, enslaving all creatures that crossed her path, and forcing them to bend to her every whim.

She wished that Creya could see her now, with her empire of shadows and slaves of the night...but thinking of her beloved sister made her feel deep pangs of loneliness. She looked around for some creatures to keep her company, but her slaves feared her smug wrath and only stayed with her if forced to. She stared around in all directions, but no free creatures were anywhere to be found...

Suddenly, she was hit with a painful realization. It had been a great long while since deer walked alongside her, birds merrily flew around her, or chipmunks rested happily on her shoulders. She may have had a full empire of slaves, but she had no friends.

To combat her loneliness, she decided to journey in search of her beloved Creya. Perhaps Creya would see the beauty and comfort of her dark empire and want to stay. Creya, after all, would never turn her back on her...

Deyja knew that she would never find her sister wandering around in the moonlight, so she set out at sunrise--the first sunrise she had seen in ages. The blazing light pierced painfully into her eyes and burned her pale flesh...but she pressed on. Any amount of suffering would be worth it to see the sweet turquoise eyes of her sister.

Creya, on the other hand, had experienced Akelian in a different light. In her time away from Deyja, she had rejoiced in the beauty of the sunlight and danced happily in green meadows, drinking in

as much of the radiant light as she could.
Though her beauty was equal to her sister's,
with silky platinum hair and captivating
turquoise eyes, she never felt herself to
be superior to the rest of the creatures. In
fact, she loved them all dearly, wanting
nothing more than to be their equal--their
friend. She spent her days sitting with the
lonely, wiping the tears of the sad, and
comforting the afraid. Through her travels,
her kindness and respect had earned her the
trust and friendship of the rest of the world.
She beamed with delight each and every day
as many different creatures wandered by her
side, not enslaved or afraid, but joyful and
free.

Deyja finally found her sister in the
very same endless fields where they had
separated so many years before. She ran
toward Creya with delight, finally reaching
the one thing her heart had desired for so
long...but she stopped suddenly just out of
sight, frozen by what she saw before her.

Creya was lying under the noon sun,
napping peacefully with the tall grass
towering over her body. A bobcat and a

deer rested contently on either side of her, napping the afternoon away, and a rabbit had curled up on her belly and was twitching slightly from a dream.

Deyja's delight melted into fiery rage as the stinging poison of jealousy flooded her veins. Anger seeped into her heart, burning like fire in her chest. Why did the creatures offer their companionship to Creya, but not to her?

Without saying a word, Deyja turned away from her sleeping sister. She began to wander the fields, lost in deep thought. Unable to see that it was her own cruelty that drove away the animals, Deyja began to suspect that nature gifted Creya with a beauty or wisdom beyond that of her own... and her love of Creya vanished under the bitterness surrounding her soul.

There has to be a way to right this injustice, she thought to herself--and revenge had suddenly become a welcome thought. After all, Deyja was the most beautiful and important creature in all of creation. Compared to her, Creya simply did not deserve the loyalty of the other creatures.

She would have to take their loyalty from her by force.

Hidden under the shadows of the night that she loved so dearly, she formulated a plan...

***

"Wait... 'by force'?" Demetri blurted out. "What in Akelian does that mean?"

"What do you think it means? She's going to kill her," said Darion matter-of-factly.

"But they're twins! You mean to tell me that just because Creya took a nap with some friends, Deyja just lost her marbles and decided to kill her?! That doesn't make any sense," Demetri argued indignantly.

Gema patiently tried to explain. "Loneliness and jealousy can make people do horrible things, Tree, things that you couldn't even imagine. I assure you, this is not as bizarre and uncommon as you might think,"

"So elves just go around killing each other when they get jealous or lonely?"

"Of course not, Tree," she said. "For one, I haven't finished the story, so you're both jumping to conclusions. Don't worry about something until you need to. For another, there are good elves and bad elves, Tree, just like there are good humans and bad humans. I don't want you walking around this world thinking that the elves are infallible, okay?"

Demetri fell silent, feeling as though the world he thought he knew was all wrong. He had always thought of elves as sort of guardians, the picture of all that was good and pure in this world. Were elves really just as evil as people?

"So they're just...human?" he asked apprehensively.

"No, Tree. They're elves. They are the closest beings to the spirit of nature on this earth, and as such are the most intelligent beings that have ever lived. Most elves are everything that you think they are, sweetheart," she smiled gently. "But don't ever assume that everyone in a group is the same. Not all humans are bad, and not all elves are good. Look at the person, Demetri, not the group."

He stared at her, feeling slightly dejected and humiliated, but not sure what to think at all.

"So, Deyja was formulating a plan..." said Darion, motioning for Gema to continue.

"Ah, right," she said as she scanned for her place.

***

Morning came quickly in the forest, but this time, Deyja almost welcomed the breath of day. The light was worth it if it brought her the sweet taste of revenge. She knew that Creya would have to wander into the woods to look for food--and she was ready for her. From a high tree branch, she watched as Creya wandered right beneath her, headed toward a waterfall. Swiftly and silently, Deyja followed...

In the blink of an eye Deyja sprang at her, plunging a sharpened stick into her once beloved sister's back.

There were no screams, no wails, no howls of pain--just silent gasps for air...

Creya looked into the eyes of her twin with heartbroken disbelief--tears fell down her face as her blood spilled onto the forest floor.

Deyja dropped her bleeding sister unceremoniously onto the ground, without the slightest hint of regret in her eye.

"Now I will be the companion of all creatures. All will honor and obey me, or else suffer my wrath!" She knelt down to hover over her sister's blanching face until she was mere inches from her. "And you?" Deyja whispered with a malicious smirk. "You will be ripped apart by my starving legions of wolves. How poetic. Your body will fill the bellies of the animals you so greatly love."

Suddenly, a fierce shriek filled the air and a swift, angry wind came down upon the sisters. Deyja looked up to see a giant snowy owl flying straight toward her. Stumbling back in fear, she tripped in her haste to get away. The massive owl, at least a foot taller than the girls, landed gently beside Creya. He turned to Deyja, and his violent amber eyes pierced right into her soul. Malice and rage burned furiously in those eyes, making

her knees buckle. Without sparing a thought
for the sister dying by her hands, Deyja fled
for the shadows of the forest--and never
looked back.

The owl's gaze returned to Creya's body,
lying helplessly in a pool of her own blood
with her last breath hauntingly close--but
she was still breathing. With a comforting
hoot, he gently lifted Creya and cradled her
frail body in his wings. Mere seconds later,
light illuminated his gentle wings, filling the
land with a soft golden glow. The blood on
his wings rapidly returned to her body, as
if it were being sucked back in. Creya found
that she could open her eyes, so she did.

The majestic owl stared at her, hooting
softly. Carefully, she rose to her feet, leaning
on the owl's wings, which were illuminated
no more. Not a single drop of blood remained
on the ground, and the gaping wound in her
back was completely healed without even a
scar. Her breath felt light and easy, and she
found that she had strength. She turned to
the owl and hugged him tightly, sobbing.

Though the owl departed Creya's side,
he left behind an incredible gift. The wings

that saved her life also imbued her soul with their very same ability: the ability to heal. With that gift, she became the first white light in existence. Her kindness and compassion brought great peace to all the creatures of Akelian. Thanks to them, despite the devastating loss of her sister, she never had to feel alone again.

Deyja, the first black light to ever walk the earth, was never seen again. She wandered aimlessly, nurturing her vanity and self entitlement, never answering to anyone but herself. From that moment on, the black lights were well known for their evil ways...and well feared. Never were they gifted a kingdom to celebrate the dark shadows and deep night. Never again did a black light have an empire built on imprisonment and fear...and never again did a black light have a place to call home.

***

All three sat in a pregnant silence for a moment before Darion finally spoke.

"Now *that*," he pointed at the book, "was awesome."

Gema beamed.

"That was disturbing," Demetri argued.

"Why disturbing?" Gema asked lightly.

"She was her twin...I mean, things got so bad between them that she wanted to kill her twin...you can't just kill your *twin*." He said, looking sincerely at Darion. "I mean, I would never--"

"It's just a story, Tree," Darion interrupted. "Plus, even if it wasn't, they were crazy twins! One spent all her time talking to animals, and the other was a power crazy psycho. Pretty serious mental defects running in that family." He smiled at Demetri and laughed brightly, but all Demetri could manage was a weak smile.

Darion looked him dead in the eye. "That would not happen to us--not ever."

Demetri felt his heart lighten as he looked into his brother's eyes, seeing his genuine smile. He smiled with misty eyes as Darion put his hand on his shoulder.

"It couldn't. I'm stuck with you. I can't leave you alone for even a few seconds without you getting hurt. Do you know how many times you would injure yourself if I didn't stick with you? Pssshhh...you'd be dead in a day."

Demetri knew that his brother was mocking him, but he laughed right along with him.

"You're not stuck with me. I would be just fine," Demetri said confidently.

"This morning you fell through a floor because of a lizard."

"Because you told me I would die if they bit me."

"And you honestly believed that?" said Darion, laughing mockingly.

"I was three!" Demetri said. "And anyway I know that it's not true now. I'm just scared of them out of habit I guess--"

"About that lizard, Demetri," Gema interrupted calmly, and both of them fell silent. "Did he deserve to die?"

Demetri thought long and hard. Images of Creya and Deyja were still fresh in his mind. He thought of Creya and the happiness she found in the end--he thought of Deyja and her cruelty, leading to a life alone--

"No," he said. "It's a living thing as well, and I should respect it. It has just as much right to be here as I do."

Gema beamed with pride. "That's my boy. Now, who's hungry?" she asked as she slowly rose from her chair, tenderly folding the book into her arm. "And don't put too much pressure on that ankle, Tree," she vaguely shook her finger at him while shuffling through the front door. "How about cheese? Yes, cheese sounds lovely right now--cheese and some nice bread..."

Both boys smiled as Demetri was helped up by his brother. Together, they made their way into the kitchen to enjoy some cheese and bread with their crazy grandmother.

Sacred Fire

"Finally!" Demetri cheered as he examined his ankle, carefully rolling it around but feeling no pain.

Darion looked up from his eggs and toast. "Feeling better?"

"Oh, yeah!" said Demetri, jumping slightly to show how well his ankle was holding up. "I can finally make the walk back to the hideout!"

He smiled gleefully as he took his place at the kitchen table, scarfing down his eggs with lightning speed. Nothing was going to stop him from getting to the hideout today.

It had been weeks since the last time he could make it out there thanks to his stupid ankle being all swollen and annoying, taking much longer to heal than Dad thought it would.

"We've got so much to do--thanks Mom," he said as she set a glass of berry juice in front of him. "We've gotta finish the floor and the railings, plus the rope ladder. And we're almost out of time." He gazed out the back window at the trees in the distance, adorned with leaves fading to a greenish yellow.

"Oh, I'm sure you'll get it done in no time," said Gema absentmindedly as she picked the end of her long hair up and off of the floor, tucking it under the green blanket in her lap. Darion simply nodded his head in agreement, not looking up from his eggs.

"Definitely," Dad chimed in, gulping down some fresh, hot tea. "The first autumn rains should hold off for at least another couple of weeks."

"Awesome," Demetri said as he hurriedly jumped up from the table and put his empty plate in the sink, ready to change clothes and head straight out to the hideout clearing. *Today is going to be a great day*, he thought to himself excitedly as he pulled some pants on, gazing out his bedroom window into a clear blue sky. Maybe his bad luck was finally over.

He ran back into the kitchen to grab Darion and say a quick goodbye to Mom and Dad, but Darion was still slowly working through his plate of eggs.

"Would it kill you to move faster than a snail's pace just once?" Demetri said bitterly, folding his arms and tapping his foot on the floor impatiently.

"Just because you're in a hurry to go on an hour long hike and then do backbreaking construction all day doesn't mean I have to be. Plus, Mom is making honey biscuits. *Honey biscuits*, Tree!" He was practically drooling. "Biscuits are going into my belly and not even a hurricane could stop that from happening."

Demetri snorted and rolled his eyes as he leaned up against the wall, arms still crossed, determined to stare Darion down in an attempt to make him eat faster.

"Feel free to go on ahead," Darion said as he shrugged his shoulders, not the least bit phased. "I'll catch up."

"It's not as much fun to walk out there on my own," Demetri whined and gave in, slumping into his chair at the table with the intent of waiting not-so-patiently for his brother, who was obviously made of molasses. There was a bright side to this delay though, however much Demetri didn't want to admit it. Mom's honey biscuits really were delicious, and they kept well during long hikes. They could set out with a pack full of biscuits, dried deer meat and carrots, and not have to return until just before the final sunlight. Maybe they could make up for their late start by staying all day instead of coming back home for lunch.

The tantalizing smell of sweet bread rose from the fire, arousing Demetri's appetite and allowing him to forget his haste for a moment. Mom smiled as she set a massive plate of biscuits in the center of the table and watched as every member of the family grabbed three at a time.

"There are plenty for you two to take with you today," said Mom with a kind smile. "And you as well when you go hunting, Jil." She leaned over Dad as he sat stuffing his face like everyone else, wrapped her arms around his bulky shoulders and kissed him on the cheek.

"Time and place, Mom," Darion teased as he rose from his chair and put his empty plate in the sink. Demetri jumped up out of his seat.

"I still have to put my shoes on," Darion reminded him. "And we'd get there a lot faster if you would stop being so thick-headed and wear shoes yourself."

Demetri rolled his eyes impatiently. "Let's just *go*."

Darion grabbed his shoes from the bedroom and threw them on quickly, probably just to placate his brother, but Demetri appreciated the speed all the same. They kissed Mom and Gema, hugged Dad, and headed for the front door. Demetri finally put his hand on the doorknob, ready to start the journey toward a full day of accomplishment and progress--

BOOM!

An earth shattering clap of thunder pounded though the air. Demetri shot Darion a distressed look before sprinting to the living room window and ripping open the curtains.

"NO!" he shouted in disbelief, pounding his fist on the windowsill as he looked out. Deep gray clouds were taking over every inch of what had been a clear blue sky only moments ago. Rain began pattering violently on the roof as Darion walked over to the window, assessing the situation. Demetri couldn't see anything through the harsh onslaught of rain, falling hard and fast as the wind whipped around in all directions. He hung his head, accepting harsh reality as Gema shuffled over to the window.

"Goodness me," she said empathetically, "It seems as though your father was a bit off about the autumn rains."

From the doorway between the kitchen and living room, Dad let out a heavy sigh. He seemed to be listening to the pounding rain with dread.

"Well, rain or shine, this family has to eat," he said heavily. After kissing Mom on the cheek, he crossed the living room, grabbed his crossbow, and made his way to the front door.

"Keep your chin up, Tree. Your hideout will get done eventually. Don't worry," Dad said, giving Demetri one last consoling grin as he stepped out the door and began trudging carefully through the thick veil of rain.

"Yeah, right," Demetri grumbled, flopping onto the couch with a bit more melodrama than he intended, but he didn't care. He was well within his right to sulk.

He could hear dishes clinking and water splashing in the kitchen, and he sank further into the couch; the scowl on his face deepened. *That's just what I need right now*, he thought sarcastically, *another day of doing dishes or laundry or whatever other pointless chores.* He couldn't imagine how he would ever get done with the hideout now.

Gema shuffled back toward the kitchen for a moment and returned carrying a plate piled with a massive mound of biscuits, some of them toppling to the floor as she made her way to her rocking chair by the fireplace.

"I don't envy your father right now," she said as she chose a biscuit and gobbled it up quickly, getting biscuit crumbs all over her green blanket in her lap. Darion nodded his head in agreement, still examining the storm though the window.

"Demetri!" Mom shouted from the kitchen. "Can you get a fire going for me?"

But Demetri just sat there like a statue, still brooding. Darion looked over to him from the window, waiting for him to get up, but he didn't budge. Darion sighed, crossed the living room, and gently patted Demetri on the shoulder.

"No worries, Tree. I've got it." He walked out of the room, leaving Demetri feeling slightly ashamed of himself.

"Wat wong tee?" said Gema.

"You need to write a book," he scoffed. "Give us some reference material on how to understand your full-mouth speech."

But Gema just chucked and gave an enormous swallow. "I was asking you what is wrong. Why do you seem so glum?"

Demetri looked at her, unable to work out why she would ask something so blatantly obvious. "Is it really not that clear? I've been trying to get my hideout done all summer, and there's always some stupid reason that I can't." He held up his hand and started ticking things off on his fingers. "It's too dangerous to work at night, we got lost every time we went to the clearing for the first three weeks, then I hurt my arm and anyway Darion wouldn't go because..." his voice seemed to get lost somewhere in his throat. Having no desire to talk about Amphy, he shook his head and continued. "Then Dad got sick and we had to help Mom with the house stuff, then I hurt my ankle because of that stupid lizard. And now--" he pointed irritably at the window, falling silent. What would Gema care? Or Mom, or Dad for that matter. The grown-ups would never understand why having a secret, awesome fort just for him and Darion was so important.

"I just..." he mumbled with a sigh, feeling slightly embarrassed. "I just want some

place special, you know? Somewhere for me
and Darion to call our own."

At that moment, Darion re-entered
the living room, clumsily trying to juggle
fire logs in his arms and a cloth sac on a
drawstring hanging from his shoulder. Still
feeling guilty about before, Demetri jumped
up and relieved Darion of some of the logs
and the cloth sac, setting them on the floor
beside the fireplace. Darion pulled some
dried leaves and sticks out of the sac, which
was full of the dry materials Dad always
brought home to help start fires. Darion
carefully placed the tinder in the fireplace
and grabbed the two fire starting stones
from the mantle.

Demetri sat in the floor and watched,
without really looking. Rain pounded on the
rooftop, serving as a sour reminder of exactly
why they were prisoners of the cottage for
the day, and for who-knew-how-long after
that.

"You know," Gema chimed through a
surprisingly empty mouth. "This reminds me
of someone. Someone who was looking for his

own special place to call his own, but he just couldn't seem to find it."

"Who?" Demetri asked curiously. It was nice to hear that he wasn't the only one to have such obnoxious luck. She winked at him, her mischievous smile spreading from ear to ear as she slowly rose from her chair, handed her plate of biscuits to Demetri and shuffled out of the room with her green blanket wrapped around her waist. Demetri jumped up from the floor and claimed a seat on the couch.

"What's the betting that she comes back with the book?" he asked Darion gleefully, watching smoke rise steadily from the fireplace. Darion busily added some more tinder as flames began to flicker.

"I'm not making a bet that I'm definitely going to lose. Besides--" he turned to glare at Demetri. "--listening to elvish tales sure beats watching you sulk all day."

Demetri opened his mouth to retort, but Gema shuffled back into the living room. Sure enough, she had the old book tucked into her arms. After adding a log to the fire,

Darion took a seat beside Demetri on the couch.

"Well, we may not be able to sit on the front porch, but that doesn't mean we can't read a story from in here," Gema said as she sat in her rocker and began thumbing through the pages.

"Now let me see..."

Her hand stopped on a page with a small picture at the top. Demetri leaned forward in his seat to get a better look. It was a simple sketch of a fire, a small, seemingly insignificant fire on a stone column. Gema looked at each of the twins in turn. "The story of The Sacred Fire, and Beanen's quest..."

***

There was never such a paradise as Akelian, nurtured lovingly by the gentle elf, Creya. Trees grew taller under her care, plants bore more fruit, and birds and beasts alike lived long, peaceful lives. The spirit of nature had remained in perfect balance for hundreds of years, all thanks to the kindness of the beautiful elf with sweet turquoise eyes. Creya had become the greatest blessing of Akelian, and it was time the land gave her something in return.

On the night of the summer solstice, in the deep forest, Creya gave birth to four beautiful elvish babies, two sweet little boys and two tiny girls. She tenderly named her girls Altrea and Leanel, and her boys Haewen and Baenen, smiling brightly at the sweet faces sleeping soundly in her arms. Creatures came from all over Akelian to see the wondrous new elves in their first few days of life, rejoicing at the sight of such wonderful blessings. Creya laid her four babies in a bed of soft grass, smiling as she gazed at them with joy.

The children grew up under the watchful eyes of not only their mother, but of all of the creatures in Akelian. They ran and played happily in the forests, frolicking with deer and chatting with the chipmunks, but they all dreamed of one day finding a special place in Akelian to call their own.

Once the children were old enough to start their own adventures, they all set out on their own separate journeys, ready to make that dream come true. Creya smiled and waved at her children as they disappeared through the trees, yet Baenen had stayed behind. She turned to her raven haired son as he stared at her with his deep brown eyes, looking lost and melancholy.

"What troubles you, my dear? Do you not wish to find your own home?" Creya asked, taking his hand.

"More than I could ever describe, Mother. Yet I am troubled, for I know not where to look. I do not even know where to start," he said with shame.

But Creya just smiled at him and squeezed his hand. "Follow your heart, my son, and you will find what you seek."

Baenen smiled weakly in return, hugged her one last time, and began his long journey. After just a few steps, the comforting voice of his mother echoed from behind him, singing a sweet tune with the same words over and over again.

"Follow your heart, and find your soul. Follow your heart, and find your soul."

***

BOOM!!

Thunder clapped loudly all around them, making the cottage shake violently and everyone jump in their seats. Demetri held his fingers in his ears to try to get them to stop ringing.

"Blimey!" exclaimed Darion, jumping up and heading towards the window. Gema held her hand over her chest, her breathing slightly labored. The color in her face was gone.

"You okay, Gema?" Demetri asked, worried.

"Oh yes, dear," she reassured him with a smile. "It's been quite some time since I've experienced thunder like that, and the last time I did wasn't pleasant at all."

Demetri returned her smile, but he couldn't help wondering if she should try to lie down. Dad always said not to jump out at Gema or startle her in any way. Demetri never really understood why, but she was clearly startled now.

"We're lucky the glass didn't break," said Darion, running his fingers around the edges of the window. "The lightning must have hit just on the other side of the tree line."

"Oh, that glass should be the least of your worries, Dare," Gema said breathlessly, some color returning to her cheeks. "All of the windows of this house were forged in the fires of Rhodarion, and are as such unbreakable."

Demetri gasped, beaming with excitement. He rushed over to the window that he had seen hundreds of times, examining it as if it were a gift just given to him.

"Really? They can never, *ever* break?" he asked, astounded.

"Not even if you took an ax to them," she said confidently.

"How do we have *elvish glass* in *our* house?" Darion asked with wide eyes, clearly gob smacked.

"That's my little secret, Dare," she winked. "Now, shall we continue our story?"

Both boys nodded their heads silently, and Gema continued.

***

Finding a special home proved almost simple for Baenen's other siblings. Haewen, the eldest, was thin and small with brilliant blond hair and blue eyes. He was a very calm and passive soul who found peace and comfort in tranquil waters. With this in mind, he journeyed to the south-east and found a beautiful bay of cool, clear water, hundreds of miles wide. He joyfully built a floating home and sailed out to the middle of his water world. He named it Mer Anemos, or "sea wind".

Altrea, the second eldest, was strikingly beautiful with a slender body, fiery red hair and captivating green eyes. She was a very intelligent young girl that preferred to remain out of sight, which proved very difficult with her bright red hair. Unlike Haewen, she decided to travel as far north as she possibly could in search of thick forests. Finally, she came to the brilliant white cliffs of the north. With peace flowing into her heart, she built a house high in the hidden treetops of the forested cliffs. She named her quiet paradise Aleodyn, or "old earth".

Leanel was the tallest of the four siblings, despite being the youngest. With sandy brown hair and honey yellow eyes, her kind face brought her many friends and close companions. She was a very cheerful soul that loved to bring happiness to all that crossed her path, but it was her love of the warm sun that led her on a quest toward the east. She stepped foot onto the soft emerald grass of a massive meadow, where miles and miles of grass stretched out as far as the eye could see. With no trees or mountains to block its rays, the bright, playful sun landed right on her face, warming her soul. Great delight filled her heart as she built a comfortable home among the tall grass. She named her sun filled land Solaurhia, or "yellow light of the sun".

News of his siblings' fortune reached Baenen during his own arduous travels. His heart filled with joy for them, yet despite the ease in which his siblings had found their homes, Baenen had been much less fortunate. He searched and searched, trailing thorough deep forests, climbing steep mountains, and even battling raging rivers...but he found nothing. None of the lands that he traveled through, no matter how glorious, were good enough for him to call home-- He had no love for hiding in deep woods and caves, the sun hurt his eyes, and as for the water...Baenen could not even swim.

And yet, he had a special relationship with fire. The simple burning flames spoke to his very spirit and soul, how something so beautiful could be so powerful, and if in the wrong hands, so horribly destructive. Yet in the darkness, fire would always bring light. To Baenen, fire was hope, a special hope that could be commanded, and he held onto the flaming hope in his heart.

On and on he went, searching and searching, repeating his mother's words to himself: "Follow your heart, and find your soul."

And yet, not even the most determined spirit can keep the demon of despair at bay forever. His heart began to feel heavier with each painful step he took, never knowing if his steps were bringing him any closer to a home.

***

"Can I point out the obvious?" Darion interrupted, raising his hand unnecessarily.

"What is the obvious, Dare?" Gema asked patiently as she held her place in the book with her thumb.

"Why doesn't this guy just go live in a volcano? I mean, bit of a no brainer there." He was unable to stop himself from smirking. Demetri just looked at him and rolled his eyes. Obviously Baenen couldn't just live in a volcano...could he?

"That does makes sense, Dare," Gema agreed. "Why don't you go find one?"

Darion looked thoroughly confused.

"Uh...because I don't have any sort of idea where one is?" he retorted with a snarky that-should-be-obvious air to his voice.

"Exactly," Gema said. "And neither did Baenen. So shall we read on?"

Darion had no reply as Gema's eyes fell back to her page.

***

In an attempt to raise his spirits, he decided to journey to the east in search of Leanel, who was not only his sister, but also his dearest friend. Though she seemed immensely happy to see him, hugging him tightly the moment she saw him, her words brought Baenen no comfort.

"Tis better to have a mediocre home than to not have one at all," she told him as they wandered the endless sunny meadows of her glorious kingdom. He looked at her, seeing the content smile that brightened her face as she surveyed her beautiful lands. His eyes fell to the ground, staring at his feet moving below him.

"Leanel," he whispered wistfully. "You gaze upon your rippling grassy meadows with great joy, and you rejoice in the warmth of your sun. This is your home, Leanel. This is where you belong." He turned to face her. "I want to belong somewhere. I want a home--and there has to be one out there somewhere, just waiting for me. I...I just have to keep looking. I will find it, as long as I don't give up."

She smiled and hugged him tightly. For many months he wandered alongside Leanel, drinking in the pleasure of her company--but his blissful reprieve could not go on forever.

After a farewell embrace, Baenen departed the beautiful land of Solaurhia and his beloved Leanel. Cold, lonely, and feeling very empty, he decided to venture toward Mer Anemos, hopefully finding some promising land along the way. Many years had passed since he had been in the presence of his eldest brother, and the promise of companionship at the end of he journey would give him the strength to keep going, when the cold, lonely nights closed in around him...

The sun faded into the west as Baenen continued to wander, wondering if he could have been turned around somewhere along the journey, and could now be heading in the wrong direction. He had been expecting to run into the white sand beaches of Mer Anemos, but somehow, he was surrounded by large, exotic plants, and the air felt hot and muggy.

Suddenly, he began to feel a stinging splash on his raven hair. Faster and faster the rain fell, until he could no longer see in front of him. He ran aimlessly, hoping to find anything to shield him from the downpour--

With a fierce strike of lightning, the silhouette of a humongous mountain caught his eye. Slipping in the softening mud, he trekked toward it in hopes of finding a cave or some sort of shelter.

Harsh thunder pounded all around him, lightning crashed everywhere in blinding strikes, and the wind whipped with all its might. Baenen continued to climb clumsily in the moss and mud--

***

"Hah!" Demetri shouted. Gema turned to look at him, looking slightly confused.

"Care to share with the rest of us?" Darion requested with a smirk.

"He got messed up by a storm too! See? It's such a horrible fate that they even have legends about it. This storm is a tragedy!"

Darion rolled his eyes and scoffed. "Oh, yeah," he said with thick sarcasm. "There will be ballads about the day poor little Demetri was cooped up in the house."

Demetri shot him a grumpy look and folded his arms, sinking further into the couch.

Gema cleared her throat. "Now, where were we?"

***

Baenen continued to climb clumsily in the moss and mud, slipping and sliding as he trekked forward. With a great squish, his foot suddenly disappeared into the soft earth. He wriggled and pulled, the rain soaking him through to the bone. Grabbing his knee, he pulled as hard as he could--but to no avail. In fact, instead of feeling his foot start to break free, it felt as if it were being pulled further into the ground.

In an instant, the earth gave way beneath him, and he fell flat on his back, sliding through a thin tunnel of mud. As he slid through, he could just barely make out the veil of rain at the end--before he knew it, he was sliding down a steep slope toward the heart of the mountain, rain splattering his soaked body once again.

He felt a giant splash as he fell into some sort of pond or lake. The icy cold water flooded his throat as his head fell beneath the surface--splashing and sputtering for his life...the world around him faded into the dark...

Something slimy grazed his leg under the water, bringing him back form the darkness. The slimy thing wrapped around his entire body like a great water snake. Barely clinging onto existence, he felt his head break the surface of the water and his body land on sturdy ground. Coughing madly, he desperately gulped in the sweet air. The slimy thing released his body and he turned, shaking violently, to look at his savior.

A giant, fiery red salamander stood before him, his great head towering above. The great head of the beast lowered until it met Baenen's eyes, staring right through to his soul.

"It is not yet your time, child of fire," it whispered. Baenen watched, speechless, as it returned to the water and swam out of sight.

Breath was painful for Baenen as he lay on his back, shivering and desperately hoping for a break in the storm. Unable to stand, he simply lay there, rain pounding on his weak body, and closed his eyes.

A brilliant flash of light shone through his eyelids and made him jump up, startled. He looked through the veil of rain, squinting to try to see in greater detail. In the distance, a tiny glint of light flickered. He could barely see it, but it was definitely there, bouncing around wildly like a hyper, glowing kitten.

A mysterious feeling enveloped his heart as he stared at the light. His feet shuffled forward, eerily taking him toward it as he stared, unaware of everything around him except the beautiful faint light in the distance.

His foot splashed into the very same water from which he had just resurfaced, shocking him back to reality. The vast body of water lay between Baenen and the strange light...and there was no way to cross it...

There was nothing for it; he would have to return to the water. With haste, he glanced around for anything that could help him cross the dark abyss. He picked up a giant log not too far from him and threw it into the water. Thankfully, it floated on the surface and seemed strong enough to support him, so he swallowed his fear and slid back into the water, grasping the log for dear life.

He waded carefully through the darkness, the rain so harsh that he could barely distinguish between it and the water carrying him toward the mysterious light. Finally, after what felt like a sodden eternity, the log bumped onto a patch of land, and Baenen weakly pulled himself out of the water. Feeling as though he would never be properly dry again, he crawled toward the tiny light.

There, dancing in the middle of a charred patch of earth, was a tiny flame, glowing and flickering so merrily that it appeared to be bouncing. Rain was still pounding hard onto the land, but the little flame endured.

Baenen gazed at it in complete awe. Throughout the powerful winds and flooding rains, the little flame refused to give up--just like him. His heart filled with joy as he scooped the tiny flame into his hands, watching as it danced on his palms.

A brilliant beam of sunlight peered through the dark clouds, breaking them apart. Harsh winds calmed into gentle breezes, and the darkness of the storm was chased away by the warm light of the sun.

Still holding the flame in his palms, Baenen looked around. He was standing on an island, one of three small islands in the middle of a giant crater. He had actually made it to the top of the mountain, but upon taking in his surroundings, he realized that it was no docile mountain at all. He was standing in the crater of a dormant volcano, a crater that had been filled with crystal clear water by ages of falling rains, leaving only three small islands above the surface of this special lake.

***

"Told you," Darion said with a confident grin.

"Beg your pardon?" Gema asked patiently.

"Volcano," he said simply. "Told you."

Demetri just rolled his eyes.

"Good for you Dare," Gema said with a slightly patronizing tone, and Demetri smirked at Darion as Gema's eyes fell back to the page.

***

As Baenen gazed around such a wondrous volcano, a strange feeling flooded his heart, one that he had never felt before...it was as if...as if his heart could sing, as if it was singing loudly in his chest, the notes filling his very soul with tingling pure happiness. He looked down at the tiny flame in his hands and beamed with delight. A beautiful land that had formed on the bones of a great volcano--a flame that endured on and on, never giving up despite the constant downpour of forces threatening to destroy it--

Finally, after years and years of fruitless searching and empty hopes, Baenen had found his home.

He built a stone pillar with a silver basin on the smallest island, giving the flame a permanent home. No matter how hard it rained or snowed, no matter how hard the wind blew, the tiny little flame never lost its glow. Baenen built his grand home on the second largest island, wanting to be as close to this life changing flame as possible. The little flame had become a sacred symbol in his brand new kingdom-- the kingdom of Rhodarion, or "fire's storm".

All of his siblings visited him at his new home and marveled at such a beautiful realm. They all smiled with genuine relief and happiness for their brother. Though they all saw his mission as pointless and stubborn, they all conceded that his beautiful realm was well worth the wait and heartache. He followed his heart, and he found his soul.

***

"Rhodarion?" Darion asked curiously.

"Ah, yes, Rhodarion," Gema said with a smile, staring at the ceiling with a nostalgic glaze in her eyes.

"That's where you said our glass is from," he remembered.

"Oh, yes," she said dreamily. "The red lights, that is, the elves of fire, are very gifted in the art of glassblowing. In fact, their houses are made of giant glass bubbles that lie around the sides of the very volcano in this tale. Just imagine what that would look like from the sky-- a massive volcano with a spiral of glowing bubbles, all the way from the summit to the base..."

Demetri stared at her in awe.

"The forests of Rhodarion are nice and warm. Tropical, in fact. They call them 'The Forests under the Mountains', and everywhere you look, elegant glass sculptures decorate the beautiful landscape.

Some even wrap around trees like vines. Yet try as you may, you will never shatter any glass from Rhodarion," she concluded, leaving Demetri breathless. Even Darion seemed mystified by the thought of such a great land and such cool glass.

"Have you ever been to Rhodarion?" Demetri asked, excitement ringing in his voice. But Gema just continued to stare at the ceiling, either lost in her own thoughts or intentionally ignoring him. He turned to Darion, unsure what to do--but Darion seemed to have a question of his own.

"When you say 'red light', what exactly do you mean?" he asked.

"Well," she said, coming back to reality, "the elves are all linked with the spirit of nature in different ways, just as the four children of Creya were. Blue lights have a special connection with water--yellow lights with the sun--green light with the trees, and plants in general for that matter--red lights with fire."

"What about the white lights?" Demetri asked, mesmerized.

"Oh, the white lights are special," she mused, rocking back and forth peacefully in her chair. "They are the creatures that are closer to the spirit of nature than any other being in Akelian. Their power is unequaled by anything that ever was or ever will be again--but white lights rarely ever use their power."

"Why not?" asked Darion.

"Because white lights are creatures of ultimate peace. They use their power to heal the sick and bring harmony to the world. They spread the teachings of peace into every corner of Akelian." Gema's face was alight with a strong sense of respect.

"Have you ever met a white light? Or a green light? A blue light?" Demetri rattled off, unable to contain his excitement and the burning questions in his mind.

"I have met many elves in my time," she said simply.

"What about the black lights?" Darion asked. Gema stopped rocking in her chair and stared at him, but Demetri couldn't work out the expression on her face. Was it somewhere between fear and dread?

219

"What about them, Darion?" she asked with a surprisingly serious tone.

"Well, you mentioned all of the others..." Darion mumbled cautiously. "I was just kinda wondering what the black lights have a special connection with."

Gema closed the book and placed it tenderly in her lap, then rubbed her eyes as if straining to find the right words to say.

"The black lights...they share a connection with the darkness of this world," she finally said, though seemingly reluctant.

"So...like shadows?" Darion said in a slightly pushy tone. Demetri wondered if his brother was pressing his luck, prying into things he shouldn't be asking about.

"No," she said through her cracking voice, her eyes still focused on the book in her lap. "Any darkness. The darkness of the night, the darkness of a broken friendship, and even the darkness of your very fears."

Demetri felt his blood run cold.

"Have you ever met a black light?" Darion asked, unable to stop himself. Gema turned her head and looked out the window.

"Ah! It looks like the storm is finally slowing down a bit," she said as her serious grimace was replaced with her normal mischievous smile. "Oh, and a good thing, too. I would hate to have to swim from my bed to the breakfast table."

She chuckled as she rose from her rocking chair and shuffled toward the kitchen.

"I wonder what else we can find to snack on? It seems as though someone ate all of the honey biscuits--"

"Well, gee," said Darion, stretching as he got to his feet. "I can't think of anyone at all who could clear an entire mountain of honey biscuits in a single sitting."

Gema laughed out loud and winked at him as they made their way through the kitchen door.

Demetri rose from the couch, his mind still burning with a million questions. Why did Gema look so intense when Darion mentioned the black lights? When did Gema meet the elves she was talking about? What kind of elves were they?

As he crossed the threshold of the kitchen, he smiled at his grandmother, who

was sloppily stuffing carrots into her mouth.
All he could do was hope that one day...
maybe one day soon...she would let them in
on her great secrets.

The Cave of Erathae

The autumn rains still hadn't relented
two weeks later as Demetri lay in his
bedroom floor, staring aimlessly out the
window at the steadily falling drops of water
outside. He had a piece of paper in front of
him and a pencil in his mouth, desperately
hoping for something to draw just to break
the mind numbing monotony. It wouldn't
be so bad if they could just go outside, even
for one second. But thanks to the weather,
setting foot out the door simply wasn't an
option.

The Anbidian family had plenty of books in the house that had been Demetri's savior over the sodden weeks. Books of both human and elvish history cluttered every corner and shelf on the house, containing anything from the science of plants to the rise of Bellumor, their home kingdom. Demetri and Darion had both been reading and reading their days away--Darion tended to read books about Bellumor and human achievements, while Demetri gravitated toward the books about or written by the elves. Unfortunately, after two weeks of being stuck indoors with nothing to do but stare at a book, the pages had all started to look the same. Out of desperation just a few hours ago, Demetri had asked Mom for a notebook full of blank paper, hoping to draw something spectacular to distract himself from the boredom...but no inspiration was coming to him.

With a huge sigh, he rolled over on his back and stared at the ceiling. Darion was on his bed lying comfortably under his blankets, still reading a book. He seemed to be really wrapped up in whatever it was, but

if Demetri didn't break the boring silence, he
was sure he was going to lose his mind.

"Dare," he said with the pencil still in his
mouth, still staring at the ceiling.

"Yeah, Tree?" Darion replied, not taking
his eyes off of his book.

"Do you want to go do something?" he
said hopefully.

Darion let out an annoyed sigh as he
looked out the window at the relentless
downpour and gray skies. "Like what?" he
asked, sounding frustrated and defeated.

"I dunno," Demetri whispered, his gaze
turning to the window again as he took the
pencil out of his mouth. "Maybe we could
play a game?"

"What kind of game?" asked Darion,
folding the corner of a page to mark his
place and closing the book. Demetri sat up
and looked around the room. Dirty clothes
littered the floor along with the piles and
piles of books they had already read. A small
wooden toy chest held a few stuffed animals
and wooden figurines--but nothing that
looked entertaining or intriguing.

"I don't know," he finally said as he flopped back down on the floor, resuming his staring contest with the ceiling. "I'm just so *bored.*"

"Yeah, me too," said Darion with a sigh as he opened his book, seemingly surrendering to another afternoon of heavy reading. Normally, the boys would welcome an afternoon of heavy reading, taking the chance to venture to far off places through the magical pages of a book, or learning fascinating facts about the world they live in--but after nothing but reading for two full weeks, anyone would want to put the books down and stretch their legs. Perhaps it would be different if someone read to them--some sort of fascinating tales--

Demetri shot up from the floor with a huge smile. "Do you want to see if Gema will read us a story? From the book?"

But Darion kept his eyes on his own book. "Gema's still sleeping. Apparently she's been really stiff all morning and Mom says she's probably not going to leave her room today."

Demetri felt the smile slide off of his face as he sat down on the corner of his bed. He

glanced down at the blank piece of paper
still in the floor but threw the pencil on top
of it, giving it up as a bad job.

Just mere seconds later, faint traces of a
tense conversation echoed from the kitchen,
flooding into their room from underneath
their closed door. Darion looked over to
Demetri with a meaningful glance as he
jumped down from the bed and sprinted
stealthily to the bedroom door. Demetri
followed his lead, crouching down and
pointing his ear toward the gap underneath
their door. It was Mom and Dad, and Mom
sounded extremely worried about something.

"--can't take them out right now, Jil. It's
too dangerous."

"I'll be there to protect them, dear. Plus,
the rain will be letting up soon--"

"But how can you know that?" Mom
interrupted him. "You're always wrong about
the weather."

"Because I saw the sky, May," Dad
said soothingly. The boys looked at each
other with budding confusion as silence
fell between Mom and Dad. Finally, Dad

spoke in a deep and comforting voice, but he sounded incredibly serious.

"This is something that they need to see, May--Just trust me, okay?"

They talking about us? Demetri mouthed to Darion, pointing at himself and Darion in turn. Darion shrugged his shoulders and shook his head, making it clear that he had no better idea than Demetri did.

"Boys!" Mom shouted, startling Demetri so much that he shot up, accidentally hitting the top of his head on Darion's chin.

"OW!" Darion yelled crossly, rubbing his chin. "You idiot!"

"You jumped too!" Demetri said defensively with his hand on his head, tears of pain welling up in his eyes. "Sorry, Dare."

But Darion just let out an aggravated grunt as he opened the door and walked toward the kitchen. Demetri followed, trying to shake the pain out of his throbbing head.

They entered the kitchen to find Mom sitting at the kitchen table, worry lining her face. Dad, on the other hand, was standing by the sink with a smile, not a single hint of worry visible anywhere.

"I would like you boys to come with me," he said simply. "Go put on your green jackets. It's going to be a bit of a wet walk."

The boys exchanged looks of delight, raced into the bedroom, and began fumbling through their clothes looking for their green jackets.

"Oh, and Tree," Dad yelled from the kitchen as they were buttoning their last jacket buttons. "Put on your shoes. No arguments."

Demetri let out a whiny moan as he reluctantly grabbed them out of the back corner under his bed. On the bright side, he wore them so infrequently that they still felt new on his feet, unlike Darion's. He wore his shoes every time they went outside, so they were covered in filth and mud and were sporting holes in the thick deer-hide soles.

They returned to the kitchen in their green jackets and shoes, their blue and green eyes both alight with excitement. Finally, after weeks and weeks of cottage fever, they get to go outside and *do something*.

Mom stood and gave both of the boys tight hugs. "Mind your father now, and be careful--"

After a reassuring smile from Dad to Mom, the three of them stepped out the back door, out of the dry shelter of the cottage and into the rain soaked, slippery clearing. Rain fell steadily on their heads as they trudged through the soft ground, headed for the tree line. Demetri could barely contain his excitement as he hiked alongside Dad.

"So where are we going? Is it far? Please tell me it's a really long journey," he rambled ecstatically. Dad laughed in a booming, deep voice.

"It's pretty far, Tree. You'll be out of the house for most of the day."

Demetri squeaked with glee.

Even though they were positively beside themselves with delight, the journey proved to be extremely difficult. Within only the first half hour, Darion was already falling behind. Demetri could hear him huffing and grunting some ways behind them, trying to catch up.

Their shoes kept getting stuck in the soft mud as they slipped and slid their way through the deep forest, Dad stopping every now and then to look for the position of the sun (how he could find it through the thick clouds Demetri had no clue), making sure they were still on the right track. Every now and then, Demetri and Dad would stop for a minute, giving the breathless Darion a chance to catch up to them.

The rain continued falling steadily and without relief. Thankfully, the canopy of branches and leaves kept most of the water droplets high above them. But despite this welcome relief, they were far from dry and toasty. Demetri kept wringing his hair every few minutes, and Darion desperately tried to keep his face dry by constantly wiping it with the sleeve of his green jacket, but to no avail since the jacket itself was soaked.

Despite the cloud covered sky and thick canopy, they could see relatively well. Their great visibility coupled with the serene smile on Dad's face kept any worries of being lost far from their minds as they trekked arduously toward their mysterious destination.

Demetri and Dad reached a steep hill and stopped, panting, waiting once again for the lumbering Darion. Once he caught up, Dad smiled widely at both of the twins.

"Just up the hill," he said, pointing at the steep hill just behind him.

"Up the hill!" Demetri cheered, running haphazardly through the slick mud. Dad followed closely behind him.

"Up the hill..." Darion mumbled, heaving heavily to catch his breath. "Spectacular..."

After a slippery hike that felt more like a climb, they reached the top of the hill to find an enormous tree towering far above their heads. Dad held his hand up to tell Demetri to stop hiking, and he obeyed. Once Darion caught up, everyone took a minute to catch their breath and shake off their sodden clothes.

"So, is this what we came out here for?" Darion asked, sounding sorely disappointed. Demetri couldn't help but agree with him. Why in Akelian did Dad feel it necessary to show them a big tree? They could find those anywhere around the cottage.

"Not quite," he said. "There is one more leg of our journey..."

He pointed at the branches just above their heads, smiling impressively.

"No!" Darion protested.

"Yes!" Demetri exclaimed loudly, jumping up and down.

"You want us to climb this monster?!" Darion shouted, aghast.

"Trust me, Dare," said Dad. "It's going to be worth it."

With a sigh from Darion, the three of them began scaling the tree, Dad in the lead followed closely by Demetri, and Darion exhaustedly pulling up the rear.

"Oh, and Tree," Dad said with a grunt as he pulled himself up onto a thick branch. "Be careful. You don't want to get injured up here."

Demetri wrapped his arm around a thick branch before looking down. Suddenly, it felt as if his stomach were falling back to the ground without him. He closed his eyes for a second, hugging the branch tightly. Without warning, he felt a hard smack on the back of his head.

"Ouch! Darion!" he shouted, turning to see the face of his brother, who had caught up to him but was still trying to catch his breath.

"Don't look down, dummy," he jeered through his panting as he reached for another branch above him. "You never look down or you'll get scared."

"I'm not scared!" Demetri argued. "Dad just made me curious that's all..."

Darion snickered as he continued his ascent, Demetri climbing carefully right alongside him.

The wind began howling through the branches as they made their way higher and higher--not even Demetri had ever climbed this high before, and it took serious effort not to look down. Thankfully, the rain had finally started to ease up, otherwise they would have been washed right back down to the ground. Once they reached a thick branch, the highest one on the tree that could support their weight, Dad motioned for them to stop.

Without a single word, he pulled a large branch out of the way that had been blocking their view--and both Demetri and Darion froze at the sight before their eyes.

The forest lay far beneath them, and the trees were alight with brilliant autumn colors, stretching as far as their eyes could see. Lines of crimson, orange and yellow leaves filled the landscape of rolling hills, meeting in the distance with a pale blue sky. Rays of sunlight beamed through the gray clouds, breaking up the storm with impeccable beauty. In the distance, the rushing river that sustained their every need lay before them, glimmering in the sunshine. Demetri's mouth hung wide open as he took in the incredible sight before his eyes.

It was as if Akelian awoke this morning, and suddenly realized it was beautiful.

"Welcome to Akelian, boys," Dad's voice whispered from behind them, but their eyes would not turn away. "The land that you call home without knowing it for what it truly is--The land with more wonders and beauty than you could ever imagine."

Demetri couldn't speak. His heart felt like it was swelling, and a tingling sensation spread from his chest to his fingertips and toes. Seeing the absolute beauty and power of nature spread out before him, how it commands the landscape and governs all life forms within it...it was enough to bring any grown man to his knees. Tears welled up in his eyes as he gazed upon this world, *his* world, his majestic world from above the forest canopy under which he had spent his entire life. He wanted to turn to Darion, to see his reaction to this whole new view of the world, but he found that he couldn't look away from the staggering beauty before him. Darion still hadn't spoken at all, and Demetri was sure that he was just as awestruck.

"See the river over there?" Dad said, pointing to the river just ahead of them. Demetri nodded his head without looking away.

"That's the river that you run alongside, racing your brother and the rushing waters. It was named Paleodyra River long ago, for the great Stag of Winter himself."

"Unreal...." Darion whispered, clearly amazed beyond words. "Just...unreal."

"It's real, my son. If we could see miles and miles into the distance," he pointed straight out ahead of them, "we would see the towering white cliffs of Aleodyn, just that way." He pointed to the other side of the river--Paleodyra--

"This is the world you have lived your entire lives in thus far, without even knowing it for what it truly is," Dad said, watching a bird fly out of a vibrant orange tree some way in the distance, its calm song filling the air with peace.

"I wanted you to see what beauty we can see just ahead of us, and imagine what beauty lies just beyond our sight. Can you imagine the crystal clear bays of the Blue Kingdom? Can you see, with your mind, the emerald green paradise of Aleodyn? Or perhaps the glittering volcano of Rhodarion, speckled with the glowing homes of the elves?"

Demetri nodded.

"Those wonderful images you have in your mind--they are absolutely nothing compared to the real beauty of these realms, the majesty of this land..."

Dad put his hands on both sides of Demetri's head, pulling it around to face him, and looked him dead in the eye.

"It is my greatest hope for you two, that you will one day see these realms with your own eyes...that you will make your own adventures and tell your own tales of this great land."

Dad turned to Darion, placing his hands on either side of his head, looking him in the eye as well.

"Because there is nothing in the world like seeing this place for yourself. Get out there, as soon as you can. You will never, ever, have a more incredible or more important experience in your life, than wandering the unbelievable majesty of this world, of your world, your home."

"Gema!" Demetri shouted as he burst through the back door and bolted to the living room, still damp and tracking mud all over the wooden floor. He couldn't wait to tell her about what he saw--but the rocking chair remained unoccupied.

He popped his head around the corner of the door and into the kitchen, finding Mom sitting at the table.

"Where's Gema?" he asked.

"Where's Darion?" Mom retorted. Demetri turned around and looked back; he hadn't realized that Darion wasn't right behind him.

"DARION!" he shouted down the hallway. Darion's muffled voice echoed from the bedroom.

"Yeah?"

But Demetri just turned back to the kitchen. "He's in the bedroom."

Mom scorned. "I could have done that, Tree."

"I know, no charge," he said. "Where's Gema?"

"She's still in bed," Mom said as Demetri rushed toward Gema's bedroom. "And don't over excite her!"

He ignored her as he knocked on the door. "Gema?" he whispered.

"Oh my, come in dear," she said, her voice sounding slightly more hoarse than usual.

He opened the door to find her propped up on some pillows, and it looked as if she had been awake before he knocked on her door. Some of the rosy color had faded from her cheeks and the circles under her eyes seemed darker, but she looked otherwise content and comfortable. Demetri beamed at her as he sat on the corner of the bed.

"You'll never guess what we saw today," he said through bubbling joy, struggling to keep his voice at an inside level.

"Was it something you've never seen before?" she asked, leaning in closer.

"Yeah! And it was--wait, why do you ask?"

"Because there's nothing like seeing something for the first time. Once you've seen something once, it never quite feels the same when you see it again."

"Uh, right," he said, not having a clue what she was talking about. It must have been one of those old people things.

"We went with Dad out in the rain, and everything was super gloomy and wet, and

Darion couldn't keep up so we kept having to stop and wait for--"

Darion opened the creaking door without knocking or saying a word.

"Where did *you* go?" Demetri asked, a slight sharpness in his voice.

"The bedroom," he taunted, closing the door behind him and crossing the room to sit beside Demetri.

"I knew that," Demetri said, rolling his eyes. "But why?"

"You may be okay with sitting around in damp clothes all day, but I'm not." Darion motioned to his new, dry, and admittedly comfortable looking clothes. After running his hand down his damp pants to examine them, Demetri just shrugged his shoulders.

"They're dry enough," he said impatiently. "Anyway, Dad got us to climb a huge tree and--"

"Darion, do be a dear and grab your Gema some cheese and water," Gema interrupted, "and possibly an apple and a honey biscuit, if there are any left."

Demetri clicked his tongue impatiently as Darion retreated for the kitchen.

"Now dear, you were saying?" Gema leaned in closer to him again as he beamed.

By the time Darion returned to the bedroom with a full plate and glass of water, Demetri had already described the amazing sights that they had seen spread out before them from the top of the tree. He did his best to spare no details about the glorious sight, but he couldn't seem to find the right words to do it justice. After a while, he just sat in silence, hoping he conveyed at least some of the beauty he had witnessed.

"How wonderful," Gema finally said to him, taking the plate from Darion and giving him a thankful nod.

"It felt like we could see forever," Demetri said with an air of amazement still in his voice. "I still can't believe how beautiful it all is, and we've been living here all along and never knew it!"

"Oh, it's much more beautiful than the little bit you saw from one single tree top," she said with her eyes on her plate, choosing a particularly smelly piece of cheese. "Some parts of Akelian will make you believe you've ventured out of reality and into the realm of a strange and elegant fantasy."

"Have you seen them?" Darion asked as he scooted over to the other corner of her bed.

"Oh yes" she replied, chewing on a biscuit. "I've seen quite a few landmarks that Akelian has to offer."

"What was your favorite?" Demetri asked, still beaming with curiosity and delight. Gema swallowed and stared out of her bedroom window, looking as though she were watching old memories playing right in front of her eyes.

"Well," she said, "I have seen the towering willows of Mer Anemos, the tallest trees in the land. And what a sight they are...The canopy of their branches stretches out a mile in all directions from the trunks--can you imagine? And the leaves are so dense that the sky can't be seen from underneath the canopy...only the green tinged light filtering through the leaves."

"Wow," Demetri whispered.

"I've also seen the unequaled beauty of the white cliffs of Aleodyn, the endless

emerald hills of Solaurhia, and the tropical forests under the Rhodarion mountains,"
she added with a smile.

"So you've seen it all," Darion summarized. "Got it."

But Gema just chuckled.

"Oh no, Dare, I have far from seen it all. In fact, even with all that I have seen, I still haven't seen the most beautiful place in Akelian."

"Which would be?" Demetri pried, motioning with his hands for her to continue. He stared at the mischievous glimmer in her eyes as she reached underneath her pillow and pulled out the book, and a delighted smile spread on his face.

"Do you actually *sleep* with that under your pillow?" Darion asked

"You will never catch me more than an arm's length away from a good book," she replied as she gently opened it and began thumbing through the pages. Demetri pulled his legs up to his knees and turned to face her, his heart fluttering with excitement as she stopped on a page toward the end of the book.

"Now as I said, there's a place in Akelian that I have never had the privileged to see. No human has, as a matter of fact. It rests on sacred ground discovered a very long time ago."

Demetri shot a fascinated look at Darion, who wasn't even bothering to hide his own curiosity. Gema gazed down at the book in her lap, but looked back to the boys before reading the first words.

"Though some may say this is just a legend, most believe it to be real and true down to the very last detail. This is the story of the most important discovery in all of elvish history, a discovery that would change what it meant to be an elf..."

***

The great Creya, mother of the elvish race, lived a full and glorious life sowing the seeds of peace and joy. And yet as she stood at the brink of the high cliffs of Aleodyn, staring out serenely to the endless hills of Solaurhia, she felt her breath becoming heavier and heavier, each breath more painful than the last. In her heart she felt a strange weakness...as if she were slipping away....like she no longer belonged in this world...

She let out a long, peaceful sigh as she turned away from the beauty of Solaurhia before her, knowing what the spirit of nature next desired of her. Wrapping herself in a thin white shawl, she began to walk through the thick forests of Aleodyn, headed for its mighty heart in the middle of this enchanted forest.

In all of her great wanderings, teaching peace and harmony to all creatures, the creatures whom she wanted to see the most were her four beautiful children, whom were out in this great land and passing on her teachings in their own kingdoms--the very thought of it made her swell with joy. It was her beloved children that she wished to be with now, and Aleodyn was the home of her beautiful daughter, the great tree whisperer, Altrea.

Altrea opened the doors of her hidden castle, welcoming her mother with a surprised smile and a warm embrace. Creya returned the smile joyfully, but Altrea saw something astray in her mother's turquoise eyes--they seemed lifeless--like her soul was barely clinging to her body...

"Do not trouble yourself, my dear Altrea," Creya said serenely, seeing the worry on her face. "We shall journey to Mer Anemos, to Haewen. I wish to see my eldest son."

Altrea nodded, her vibrant red hair falling in front of her face. Although she felt uneasy about traveling with her mother in such a weak state, she wanted nothing more than her mother's happiness. After all, happiness as a whole would not even exist without her. Altrea covered her mother's shoulders with an emerald traveling cloak, and they journeyed to Mer Anemos.

After many weeks of toil, Altrea and Creya finally came upon the towering weeping willow trees of Mer Anemos, their mighty roots forming natural docks for the sea-going Haewen. After finding a small boat big enough for only two, they floated to the center of the bay to find an enormous, elegant castle adorned with seashells and painted waves under a blanket of brilliant stars. Haewen welcomed them happily, smiling as he hugged his sister tightly, his vivid blue eyes meeting her emerald green ones. As he stared into her concerned eyes, a heaviness sank into his stomach. He turned to his mother and hugged her, and he too saw something astray in her turquoise eyes...

"Do not trouble yourself, my dear Haewen," she said weakly as she took his hand, leaning on his shoulder for support. "The three of us shall journey to Rhodarion, to Baenen. I wish to see my second son."

Altrea and Haewen exchanged looks of worry, but again obeyed their mother's orders. Before departing, Haewen hung a seashell pendant around his mother's neck--a symbol for safe travel in his kingdom. He carefully helped his mother and sister into their small boat, dismissing their worries about the boat only being big enough for two. He set the boat adrift in the bay and dove into the crystal clear waters, swimming easily alongside them, his long blond hair floating elegantly through the water. He swam beside them through the

entire bay and all the way to the willow
docks, where they tied up their boat and left
it behind. Together, they trekked arduously
through the forest under the mountains,
making their way toward the great volcano
of Rhodarion.

Once they finally reached the water filled
crater at the volcano's summit, they found
the three islands joined together by bridges
of thick glass. Carefully, the three of them
shuffled across the bridge that took them
to the glorious glass castle shimmering in
the sunlight. Baenen threw the doors open
with delight and hugged each of his siblings
in turn, his raven hair tied up on the back
of his head. He stood in front of them,
drinking in the sight of their beloved faces...
but their faces held something behind the
delight of their reunion. Something dark...
deep worry and concern... Fear began to seep
into his heart as he turned to his mother,
her body trembling, her breath rattling, and
something astray in her turquoise eyes...

"Do not trouble yourself, my dear
Baenen," she wheezed, taking his hand. "We

shall all travel to Solaurhia, to Leanel. I wish to see my youngest."

Baenen exchanged looks with his siblings--looks of both worry for his mother, and anger for his siblings. How could they let her travel in such a state? But as he looked into her mother's deep, longing eyes, he found that he could not disobey her either. Conceding to the journey ahead of them, he slipped a pair of soft, flexible glass slippers onto his mother's feet, hoping to make her journey easier. Together, the four of them journeyed slowly and carefully toward Solaurhia.

The four elves stepped into the endless fields of Solaurhia and smiled at each other. Exhausted from their travels, they continued to trek through the fields until there was nothing to be seen but grassland all around them and the beaming sun high above them. They found a vast network of above ground tunnels stretching like a great maze through the fields, but hidden under the tall emerald grass--the home of their youngest sibling, the kind and cheerful Leanel.

After bouncing and beaming through the maze of grass and tunnels, Leanel welcomed her whole family with arms thrown wide open, pulling her siblings into a huge embrace. But as she stared into the despair-lined eyes of her siblings, confusion filled her heart. She turned to her mother and saw a frail elf in front of her, platinum hair dull and lifeless, hands trembling, knees wobbling, hardly any breath through the heavy rattling of her lungs--and something astray in her turquoise eyes...

Suddenly, Creya collapsed into Leanel's arms, and Leanel let out a shocked gasp. Carefully, she led her mother toward a soft bed of grass inside her home and gently helped her to lie down, her three siblings following her closely. Leanel searched the faces of her siblings for any sign of hope or happiness, but she could find no trace. Fear and pain seemed to have swept their joy away long ago...when their mother came to visit them...so frail...

Lying upon Leanel's comfortable bed, Creya stared into the concerned faces of her four beautiful children. She lay, shaking

and feeble--but she did not weep, she did
not wail, she never even shed a tear. She
simply smiled her serene, peaceful smile as
she summoned up a little bit of her strength,
and spoke calmly to them, her four beautiful
babies, born to her in these very fields...

"My dear children, you are the greatest
gift that nature has ever gifted me, and I
am eternally grateful for the simple gift of
your love." She breathed a heavy sigh and
closed her eyes for a moment, gathering
more strength. "You have each shown your
unconditional love to me on this journey,
that you are willing to make heavy sacrifices
for the happiness of another--for my
happiness. Your sacrifices and compassion
fill me with great pride. One day very soon,
I will leave the fate of Akelian to you, and I
will have no fear. For I know that you will
continue the legacy of peace and kindness in
my absence..."

The four siblings exchanged looks of
horror and confusion, each waiting with
bated breath. After a moment of tense
silence with Creya breathing weakly through
her rattling chest, she finally spoke.

"My time in Akelian is nearly at an end. It is time for me to die."

***

"Hold on," Darion said, sounding confused. "She's dying? Like--" he drew an ominous line across his throat and retched, sticking out his tongue, "--dying?"

"Well, yes," Gema said, chuckling slightly at his expression. But Darion just shook his head as if what she said made absolutely no sense. To be fair, Demetri was a bit confused himself.

"But the elves live forever, don't they?" Demetri asked, cutting off Darion just before he spoke. Darion let out a loud huff of annoyance.

"Oh, that's a common misconception among us humans," said Gema as she leaned forward, holding her hand to the side of her mouth as she whispered, "But I have a secret, if you're willing to hear it."

Demetri sat straight up, nearly falling off of the edge of the bed in his haste. He looked over to Darion who simply rolled his eyes, leaning closer to Gema as she began to whisper.

"The elves are not immortal. They too succumb to death, just like every other living thing in this world."

She smiled, seeming very proud of herself as she leaned back onto her pillows--but their confusion hadn't wavered in the slightest. In fact, now Demetri felt even more lost than he had before.

"Wait, then why do the humans think they're immortal if they aren't?" he asked.

"Simple," she replied, "The elves live for ages and ages, up to one thousand years."

Both boys gasped loudly.

"Oh yes," Gema said, nodding slightly. "One thousand years and one day, on average."

"One thousand years?!" Demetri yelled a little louder than he had intended.

"And one day," Gema repeated. "They also never age past twenty-five years. So you see, a human could meet an elf in his early childhood, meet that same elf again as an old man, and the elf would appear exactly the same. Humans can be quite forgiven for thinking that elves are immortal."

Demetri's jaw was still hanging open as the word "Wow" fell out of his throat.

"So..." Darion said cautiously, "Did that happen to you?"

Gema looked taken aback. "I beg your pardon?"

"Well," Darion looked over to Demetri as if asking him to back him up. "We all know that you've met elves before in your life. Did you meet an elf and know her for a long time, and never see her age?"

Gema glanced out of the window for a second, as if the answer to Darion's question would suddenly fly up and land on the windowsill. Finally, she simply said, "Perhaps," flashing them a mischievous smile. "Shall we read on?"

***

News of their mother's impending death rang frightfully in their ears. Altrea broke into silent tears and covered her face with her hands, her fiery hair shielding her sorrowful simper from the others. Haewen wrapped his arms around her and stroked her hair. Unable to hold back his own tears, they fell shamelessly onto her shoulders. Baenen closed his hand around sweet Leanel's, unable to do anything but watch as she stared at their mother with deep confusion; her honey yellow eyes seemed incapable of understanding such sorrow.

Creya saw the despair and confusion in her children, and her serene smile faded.

"Do not trouble yourselves, my children," she wheezed. "Death, after all, is simply a part of life that we all must experience. From the most cold and cruel at heart to the most pure and good, from the smallest ant to the largest tree, all will perish one day, including all of you." She looked into the eyes of each of her beloved children, and her serene smile returned to her face as she whispered, "One day, you will all return to me--when you yourselves return to the spirit of nature."

Altrea fought back her tears as she smiled in return. Haewen and Baenen smiled weakly as well, but Leanel still stared at her in bewilderment, not letting go of Baenen's hand. Creya tenderly rolled onto her side before giving her children one last request...

"You have all found glorious and beautiful homes for yourselves, homes for you to live and die in," she said as she closed her eyes. "Find me such a place. Find me a place of beauty and tranquility, where I can rest eternally in peace."

They all nodded without question, and prepared to set out immediately. Before leaving, Leanel laid a single sunflower beside her mother, to bring her cheer until they could return. In turn, they each kissed their mother on the cheek. They were all holding back tears as they waved to her... hoping to see her again...to see her smile just one more time...

The siblings had all traveled through all of the lands of their own kingdoms, so they decided to travel to the north-west, where the mountains were seldom explored. Trying not to be slowed by the heavy burden of their grief, they journeyed solemnly but swiftly. With lightning speed, they found themselves standing in the beautiful, eerie woodlands of the northwest mountains. Altrea held her hand up, motioning for her siblings to stop and they obeyed, staring around at the land before them. The mountains had their own beauty and majesty, with high rolling hills and beautiful woodlands, but its beauty could not compare with the beauty of their mother's turquoise eyes; the gentle breeze could not compare to her gentle healing touch.

After many days of searching, Baenen let out a scream of rage, kicking a boulder with all of his might before sitting on it, holding his head in his hands. Strands of his raven hair had fallen out of his braid. Haewen put a comforting hand on his brother's shoulder as Leanel looked around, finding no comfort in her surroundings. As Altrea looked at the face of her sister, she felt like she was staring at another person. Leanel simply was not herself without her warm smile, and Altrea would have given anything to see her, or anyone, have a reason to smile again.

Worry grew like a plague in their minds... their mother did not have much longer...

That evening, a shimmering full moon illuminated the sky with a faint glow. While stoking a small fire, Haewen noticed a glowing in the distance. Curiosity taking over his mind, he rose to try to get a better look. An entire mountain was radiating the glowing light of the moon, as bright as a massive firefly. Captivated by this strange light, he ran over to his sleeping siblings, shaking them each awake in turn. When they stared at him with affronted expressions, he pointed in the direction of the mountain...so bright against the midnight sky...such a beautiful light... somehow comforting to the soul...

Without hesitation, Haewen smothered the fire and the four of them set out to find the mountain, wanting nothing more than to stand upon its moon kissed surface.

The hike was a short and simple one, leading them to the base of the mountain after mere moments. Together, they climbed arduously toward the summit, the rocky terrain proving much more difficult than the breezy hike. Rocks crumbled and rolled down the mountainside as they grabbed for them to try to pull themselves up. Leanel tried to grip a particularly heavy rock, hoping its weight would make it more stable, but the rock slid right through the ground into some sort of hole. Breathing a sigh of relief that she hadn't fallen through herself, she tried to use the hole as a foothold and shoved her foot into it.

Without warning, the ground completely gave way underneath her and she plummeted, screaming madly, into a black abyss. Baenen jumped in after her, shaking off Altrea's hands which were desperate to stop him. Altrea and Haewen exchanged brave but terrified looks before plummeting into the abyss, holding hands.

Landing on cold ground with a thud, the two elves found their siblings unscathed, but unable to look away from the brilliant sight before their eyes. Altrea and Haewen turned see the astounding sight that had captivated their other siblings--and what a captivating sight it was--

A small, glittering cave was illuminated by the light of the full moon, and white mother-of-pearl walls gleamed in the moonlight. A small hole in the roof showed the clear night sky, just large enough to allow a single ray of moonlight into the cave. Bathed in the moonlight was a small island in the middle of a pond, where a single tree with vivid green leaves had taken root. The twisted, elegant tree was both ageless and beautiful, with roots growing into the crystal clear pond which glimmered like diamonds in the moonlight. The pond met with a thin band of land in the rear of the cave, creating a shore as still and silent as stone, hidden in the shadows of the moon beams. Curvy, elegant crystals surfaced from deep underground on this little belt of land, crystals so deep underground that they glowed red, dimming and brightening with the pulsing magma heart of the earth.

It was in this cave that all of the elements of nature came together on their own--just as the siblings had always remained together as a family. Their mother helped to hold their family together, just as the white walls did for the cave-- All that was good and beautiful was present in this cave. Finally, they had found a worthy resting place for the mother of the elves, the mother of peace, the mother of harmony.

They raced back to Solaurhia as quickly as they could, refusing to stop for rest or food, hoping desperately that they weren't too late.

As they reached their mother's bed, they found her resting peacefully, breathing slowly but comfortably. Sensing their presence, she opened her eyes weakly and smiled at her children. Without them having to say a word, she knew that they had fulfilled her last request.

As quickly as he could, Baenen forged a wagon for her to lie in while they journeyed to the cave. Altrea filled the wagon with the softest grass that she could find in the fields. Haewen filled many sacs with the most clear, cool water he could find to help her hold on through the journey. Once Creya was lying comfortably in the wagon, Leanel placed many sunflowers on either side of her mother, to help keep her spirits up during the journey.

Together, they all headed toward the mountains.

After a tense and sorrowful journey, they came upon the cave during the powerful sunlight of the summer solstice. At the mouth of the cave, Haewen lifted his mother and carefully cradled her in his arms. The family entered the cave together, with solemn thoughts and heavy hearts. The sunlight revealed a whole new beauty in the cave, illuminating every detail of its magnificence. Creya stared in amazement with tears in her eyes and pure joy in her heart.

"Thank you, my beautiful, wonderful children," she wheezed heavily, gasping between words. "I will rest here in peace and tranquility...and you will always be with me."

Unable to hold back the tears any longer--the confusion, the anger, the gut wrenching pain--all of them wept.

Seeing the pain in her beloved children's hearts, she weakly spoke them, gathering the last of her strength for one final farewell.

"My wonderful children...my gifts...my blessings. Please do not weep for me. My spirit will endure in the life of the earth--in the breath of the wind through the trees--in the warmth of the sun--in the cool showers of rain--and in the burning heart of the flame. I go back to where I belong, and I will be with you always. You need only close your eyes and feel my spirit, guiding you from afar."

She looked into each of their eyes, smiling widely, filling them with as much love as she could possibly give them...knowing it would be the last time. Slowly, she closed her turquoise eyes, rested her head on Haewen's shoulder--and breathed no more.

Haewen leaned over and kissed his mother on the cheek, his tears spilling onto her shoulder as he turned toward his siblings. Each of them kissed their mother on the cheek, saying their final goodbyes through inevitable tears. They were all finally ready to let her rest.

Haewen walked into the clear pool until the water was at his waist, staring at his mother one last time. Creya, still covered in her emerald green cloak, with a seashell around her neck, glass slippers on her feet, and a sunflower over her chest, was lowered gently into the water by her eldest son.

Her face, peaceful and still smiling, became submerged under the water...Haewen released her body from his arms...

In an instant, her body faded away, disappearing entirely...the children stared solemnly into the empty pond before them. A swift breeze flowed through the hole in the roof and danced on all of their faces. They all smiled, knowing that their mother was still with them, continuing her duties from beyond. She had at last become one with the spirit of nature.

Together, the siblings placed a clear crystal on the tree at the base of its branches, in loving memory of their mother, the mother of peace and happiness. Her kindness, wisdom, beauty, and grace would live on in the cave, and in their hearts, for all eternity.

***

Gema tenderly closed the book and placed it on the table beside her bed.

"The Cave of Erathae is what they called it, that special cave," she said, smiling at the book. "It's the one place in Akelian that I would give anything to see with my own eyes."

"Why can't you?" asked Demetri, standing up to stretch his legs.

"Because she's too old, idiot," said Darion rather rudely. "She'd never survive the journey."

Gema looked affronted.

"It's okay, it's not as if I'm lying right here in front of you and can hear everything you say. Do continue, Dare." She folded her arm and stared at him sternly, but the corner of her mouth was twitching with a smile.

Darion looked slightly embarrassed and ashamed of himself. "Sorry--I just meant--we would all worry if you--I mean not that you couldn't--" he stammered, but Gema just laughed.

"Oh, don't worry my boy," she said, pulling her blankets up to her armpits. "I won't be making any long journeys or going on any crazy adventures any time soon. But that isn't why I can't see Erathae."

"Why can't you then?" Demetri asked as he sat back down on the bed.

"Erathae cave is considered sacred ground to the elves," she said with a disappointed sigh. "It lies under the protection of the most highly guarded elvish kingdom in Akelian, and no human is ever allowed to set foot anywhere near it."

Questions started coming to Demetri's brain faster than he could contemplate them. Guarded elvish kingdoms? Sacred ground? He didn't even know where to start.

"Why is it sacred?" he finally settled on.

"Because the cave is incredibly special," she began. "It is not only believed to be Creya's final resting place, the cave itself has a special purpose. You see, newborn elves are given a special clear crystal to wear around their necks. On the very day that they are born, they're taken to Erathae and placed carefully in the water, held by one of their parents. The crystal in the middle of the tree starts to glow vibrant colors--and from what I'm told, it's a wondrous sight to behold. The crystal settles on one color, showing that elf's true aura. The crystal around the baby's neck will change color as well to match the aura of the elf. So you see, green lights all have green crystals with them--blue lights have blue crystals and so on--because all elves carry their crystals with them throughout their entire lives."

She stared up at the ceiling, but seemed to be looking right through it. "I've known elves that have embedded their crystals into the hilt of swords, the buckles of belts, and even the insides of shields. I've seen some elves wear them as pendants around their necks, while others still that have made elegant bracelets. You see," she rolled over onto her side and looked down to the edge of the bed at Demetri, "to an elf, that crystal is a part of the soul--they will never be parted from it."

Demetri couldn't help but want a crystal of his very own. He looked over to Darion, who was still wearing the pendant from Bellumor around his neck...he never took it off. In a way, that pendant was like Darion's crystal, and in that moment Demetri badly wanted one for himself. Though he knew it was impossible--after all, only the elves

have auras, and only the elves are allowed to
have such special crystals--he couldn't help
but wonder what color his would be if he got
one...what color would the cave settle on for
him if he were and elf?

"Where is the cave?" he asked out loud,
but Gema shook her head.

"You won't find it, Tree," she said kindly.
"It's far too well protected."

"Why not?" he asked. Perhaps he *could*
find it himself one day. It couldn't be that
hard; he knew how to navigate using the sun
and stars, and maybe when he was older and
stronger--

The bedroom door creaked open and Mom
stood in the doorway, carrying a plate of
steaming soup and fresh bread.

"Oh, thank you dear," Gema said as Mom
set the plate on a tray in front of Gema's bed.
Mom reassured her that it was no trouble
before turning to the boys.

"You two need to let your Gema rest
now," she said as she headed for the bedroom
door once again. They both stood and
stretched their legs, and Mom flashed them

a loving smile before disappearing through the door.

"The sun is out again," Gema said, looking out the window again. "It may be a bit muddy and slightly chilly, but you boys should go play outside. It does not do well to be cooped up for too long."

"Yeah," Demetri said, leaning down and kissing her on the cheek. Darion came up behind him and did the same, then they headed for the door.

"Boys," Gema called out just as Demetri's hand touched the doorknob. They both turned to look at her.

"There is something I need you to do for me today," she said as she ripped apart her bread. They exchanged curious looks with each other before looking back at her, waiting for her request. She smiled widely with a mischievous twinkle in her eye.

"I want you both to think long and hard about tomorrow and what you want from dear old Gema. After all, you only have your twelfth birthday once."

First Contact

Dawn arrived quickly the next morning, covering the lands with pale light as lavender and pink skies began to chase the darkness away. As the sun crept higher into the early sky, its beams shined through the bedroom window of Demetri and Darion.

But Demetri was already awake, lying in his bed and watching the sun rise, waiting for anyone else in the house to finally wake up.

He couldn't sleep very well throughout the night last night. Today was, after all, a very special day--Both he and Darion were officially twelve years old.

Though he didn't feel much different than he did last night, he couldn't help the excitement tingling all throughout his body. He tossed and turned as he lay there, mustering up as much patience as he could. To keep his mind occupied, he focused on Gema's words from the night before--"I want you boys to think about what you want for tomorrow."--Well tomorrow had become today, and despite his excitement, he couldn't seem to answer her question. In the middle of the forest, days and days away from Bellumor, they couldn't just go out to the shops in the street and browse around for some new toys. *The things I want can't be bought in a store anyway*, he thought to himself and sighed, *you can't buy adventure...*

Darion snorted loudly and rustled around on his bed. Demetri shot up as Darion lazily rubbed the sleep out of his blue eyes.

"HAPPY BIRTHDAY DARION!" Demetri shouted so loudly that the windows shook.

But Darion simply grunted, squinting over at Demetri and shaking his head.

"Did you sleep at all?" he mumbled.

"I did!" Demetri said as he jumped out of bed excitedly and threw some pants on. "Just not as much as you. What do you want to do today?" He hopped onto Darion's bed obnoxiously--Darion shoved him off of the bed onto the floor, but he jumped right back up and started hopping around the room.

"Let's go outside! Do you want to race along the river? We haven't done that in a long time," he said as he stopped hopping and pulled a long sleeved shirt over his head.

"Not since you trampled on a thorny branch," Darion said through a yawn.

"Yeah yeah yeah," Demetri retorted. "We're going to the hideout at some point right?"

"I'm not going anywhere until after breakfast," Darion said with finality, finally stumbling over to his wooden chest to find some clothes.

"Oh, well that's a given," Demetri agreed. They headed toward the kitchen, Darion shuffling slowly behind Demetri.

"Happy Birthday boys!" Mom, Dad, and Gema shouted as they entered the kitchen, each one beaming at them. They smiled in return as they inhaled deeply through their noses, taking in the delightful smell of freshly baked honey biscuits.

"This is wonderful! Thanks Mom!" Demetri said gleefully, taking his seat at the table.

"It's no trouble at all dear," she smiled as everyone sat down in front of their empty plates. Before anyone had time to say anything at all, Darion had already finished two biscuits and was reaching for a third. Gema chuckled as she loaded her own plate with five biscuits, but Demetri knew that wasn't going to be enough for her endless pit of a stomach. *Seriously, how can one little old woman pack away that much food?* He giggled slightly as he grabbed a couple of biscuits for himself.

After a few minutes of comfortable silence, everyone contently stuffing bits of fluffy sweet biscuits into their faces, Demetri leaned back and rubbed his belly, letting out a content sigh. Darion let out a loud belch,

earning him a steely look from Mom, but
Demetri knew she wouldn't say anything to
him--not today.

"Well," Mom said irritably as she turned
away from Darion's do-something-about-it
grin, "the best gift I can give you two is a
day off. You both are free of your chores for
the day."

"Cool!" Demetri cheered.

"Awesome," Darion said coolly.

Gema grabbed the last two biscuits,
cramming one of them into her mouth before
she spoke. "Whach oogye dwin--"

Everyone tried--and failed--to stifle their
laughs. She gave a huge swallow and cleared
her throat. "What do you boys plan to do
with the day?"

Demetri's green eyes met Darion's
blue ones, and they both shrugged their
shoulders.

"We figured we would go outside and do
something," said Darion as he stood and
motioned for Demetri to do the same, and
Demetri bolted up with delight.

"One condition," Dad said before they could get get through the doorway. Demetri's stomach sank as he turned to look at him.

"You can't go to your hideout today, Demetri," he said solemnly. "I was hunting in that area throughout the night, and a pack of wolves is making its way through. They shouldn't stay long, but it's not safe to go out that way today. Understand?"

It felt as if someone pricked his heart with a needle and watched it slowly deflate. He nodded his head glumly and walked out the door.

The crisp autumn air made Demetri thankful that he had chosen a long sleeved shirt for the day. The scent of pine and falling leaves swirled in the air on the gentle breeze, blowing their sandy hair slightly as they jogged toward the tree line. The sky was a pristine blue with no sign of rain to dampen their special day. With his spirits high, Demetri tapped Darion on the shoulder and bolted as fast as he could for the river, hearing the leaves crunching under Darion's speedy footsteps behind him.

Their chore free morning proved to be a magnificent one, despite having to keep their distance from the hideout. Demetri stomped Darion in a head on race down the river, leaving him panting and heaving so far in the distance that Demetri could barely see him tottering behind.

After Darion was finished sulking and calling Demetri a cheater, they climbed some nearby trees and bounced wildly on their branches, giggling as they made the crimson leaves fall to the ground. They spent some time gathering a huge pile of leaves and threw themselves (and each other) into it over and over again. Demetri rolled out of the pile, grabbed a large stick and held it in front of him, pointed at Darion.

"I challenge you to a duel!" he shouted, giggling as he spoke. Darion scoffed as he got to his feet, nearly slipping on some of the more slippery leaves.

"You're on!" he said, looking around for his own stick, but Demetri had just had an idea.

"Ooh! Let's play 'elves and humans'! I'll be the elf and you be the human," he said excitedly, handing Darion the stick. "If I say a spell like 'fog comes down all around you' you have to pretend like it does."

"So...which light are you going to be?" Darion asked, waving the stick around in front of him.

"I'll be all of them!" Demetri replied, holding his hands out in front of him ready to cast a pretend spell, but Darion had just let the stick fall out of his hand.

"You can't be *all* of them," he scoffed. "That's unrealistic. No elf has all of the powers."

"Fine," Demetri conceded. "I'll be a green light so that I can make trees wrap around you and squeeze your body!"

"Oh you think your little trees can take the might of my sword?" Darion jeered, grabbing the stick and pointing it at Demetri. "My sword will cut through your trees like an ax!"

"I summon vines to swirl all around you and bind your wrists and ankles!" Demetri put his hands together and mimed vines coming out from the trees toward Darion, but Darion was fast with a sword--even a pretend one. Like lightning, he sliced wildly through the air in all directions.

"Ha!" he said, holding his stick by his side. "I have defeated your vines, you wimpy elf! Is that all you've got for me?"

Demetri laughed madly and held his hands together, ready to make some tree branches scoop Darion up and constrict him--

"DEMETRI! DARION!" Dad called out from the cottage far in the distance. Demetri dropped his hands and let out a disappointed sigh as Darion dropped his stick.

The sun was high in the sky once they got back to the cottage, sweaty and covered in dirt. Mom pointed her finger down the small hallway without saying a word, making them head to the back room to wash up. Birthday or not, there was no way Mom would allow filthy bottoms to sit in her chairs.

Once they were sufficiently clean, everyone sat down at a table laden with a glorious lunch.

"Rabbit stew with carrots and celery in it, and juicy apples on the side," Mom said with a generous smile, spooning the stew into each of their bowls as they looked on, salivating.

"So, how has your day of play been so far?" Gema asked as she swirled her stew around with her spoon. The boys launched into a long story of their silly games in between bites, sparing no detail.

"--Then we played this new game called 'elves and humans'--I came up with it--where I pretend to be an elf with awesome powers and Darion pretends to be a human with a sword and we fight each other," Demetri said as he chewed on a big chunk of rabbit meat.

"We don't really have any clue how they would fight," said Darion in a matter-of-fact tone. "So we just pretend. It would be really cool to see elves and humans fight like that though wouldn't it?"

"Oh yeah!" Demetri agreed with bubbling enthusiasm. "Like a full fledged war where all of the elves came together to fight, can you imagine? It would be so--so--"

All clanging of spoons and chewing had stopped. Mom was standing by the counter staring at the two of them, a very serious expression on her face--one of severe disappointment. Dad was rubbing his eyes with his fingers, the way he always did when he was stressed or upset. Gema stared at them with eyes as big as saucers, her hands trembling. She had a painful look in her eye, as if she were fighting back some horrible memory. Demetri and Darion looked at each other, both extremely confused.

"Boys..." Dad said seriously, still rubbing his eyes and not looking at them. "You have no idea what you just said."

The silence was so thick in the air that it felt hard to breathe. Demetri suddenly felt incredibly guilty, but he had no idea why.

"I'm...sorry?" he said, not entirely sure what he should be sorry about.

Dad lifted his head and opened his mouth to speak, but Gema interjected before he could get a word out.

"Son, let me handle this," she said. Her crackling voice was calm, but still very serious.

"Mom I don't think--"

"Son..." she repeated, this time more forcefully. "Let me handle this."

Dad exhaled in defeat, motioning for her to continue. She turned to Demetri and Darion with the same serious expression on her face.

"Come on boys, I want you to follow me." She stood shakily with help from Darion, and the three of them made their way to the front porch. Tension seemed to ooze through the front door, following them out to the front porch as they each took their normal seats. Gema looked out toward the tree line, rocking back and forth as she stared out for a few long moments.

Demetri and Darion just sat there, reluctant to break the silence or jar her from her thoughts. They glanced up at each other every few seconds, but their eyes quickly fell to the floor again every time.

"My boys are twelve years old now--" she said with a faint smile. Neither of them said anything.

"--and I believe twelve is old enough."

She sat up as straight as her frail body would let her, and both boys looked at her with tense bewilderment.

"Boys, it is time for me to read you a very important story. No, Demetri--" she said quickly, seeing the delighted expression on his face. "This is no fairy tale or grand heroic adventure."

His face fell.

"What I am about to read to you is a true story. It's absolutely real, and happened in Akelian. It's time for you boys to know why we left Bellumor all those years ago."

Demetri's heart hammered in his chest as he looked over at Darion, whose brilliant blue eyes stared at him with bitter tension. Tenderly, Gema pulled the book into her lap and opened it, flipping through to the very final pages, which, Demetri noticed, were written in a completely different handwriting than the rest of the book.

***

Of all the moments in elvish history, every corner of creation and every second of time, no moment had more impact on Akelian than this one. It was a simple moment during a simple time--but after this fateful moment, the world would never be simple again.

It was the moment an elf saw a human for the very first time...

I was just a young lad back in those days, a red light full of fire--a desire for adventure in a painfully boring kingdom. Rhodarion was a beautiful land of peace and plenty, but excitement? Well, it was as dry as a bone for that. I would often wander the borders of my kingdom, dancing on the line between familiar homes and mysterious lands, inching farther and farther into the unknown with every passing journey.

I was on one of such a journey, carelessly chewing on dried deer meat as I swaggered through forests far west of home. The sun was shining brightly and the wind blowing gently through my raven hair, making for a pleasant journey. With nothing weighing down my heart, I traveled quite aimlessly and carefree...

Then I heard it.

A rustle in the distance caused me to stop in my tracks, frozen for a long moment. As I am no green light with spectacular vision,

I could not see through the distant trees to pinpoint this strange sound, but it sounded big...really big...

With stealth as my aid, I lurked through the forests with incredible speed, yet as silent as death--swift and silent--that's how I hunt, and how I stay alive. Within no time at all, the strange creature came into my view as I lay hidden underneath a bush...and what a strange creature it was.

At first glance, I would have thought it an elf--it stood upright and had very little fur as we do--but it was much too big. Whereas our kind averages 50 inches in height, this creature was at least 65 inches or taller.

Their faces held no innocent beauty. In fact, compared to our kind, these creatures looked more akin to the monkeys from my forests. They were clearly intelligent, for they wore clothes and carried weapons. Could they even have the gift of language?

I began to wonder--and worry--if there were more of them. Could there possibly be an entire pack of these things?

Almost as quickly as I could think of those questions, more of the creatures came rustling through the brush. They were just as big as the first one--and carried just as many weapons. For the first time, lying there outnumbered four to one by weapon wielding monkeys, I began to fear for my life. I stayed as still and silent as I possibly could.

The creatures all wore the same clothing, as if it were some sort of statement of unity. Perhaps a pride of some sort?

The strange creatures all engaged in conversation, none of which I could understand. After a few moments, they nodded at each other and began walking briskly toward the western sun. Without any sort of hesitation, I followed, swift and silent.

It wasn't long at all before they reached a break in the tree line...and my very breath was stolen from me by grim horrors...

Fields and forests for miles into the distance...were gone. Corpses of trees still stood in the earth, mercilessly cut down to nothing but a dead stump, the only memorial to the murder of a great and wise creature, absorbing knowledge of the world for far longer than elves ever could...

A massive gray wall at least twenty feet high stood in the distance, the only barrier between me and the dwelling of these creatures, these...only one word came to my mind, though I knew not why...Humans.

Raging fire boiled in my blood, and I dashed as fast as a wild cat toward the great stone wall. Using specially made rope from a friend in Aleodyn, I hastily scaled this massive wall with ease, able to avoid being spotted. As I crouched at the top, the reason for the wall's existence became immediately clear.

On one side, the side that I came from, the land was abuzz with life and nature and beauty-- the other side was a festival of horror. Grey slabs of stone formed pathways between houses, large, luxurious houses also made of stone. There were no trees, no bushes, no plants at all save ones gathered for food. No sound of a bird or frog came from that side of the wall. In fact, save the humans, the only creatures were dead ones hanging from sticks, being prepared for later meals. The colorless streets formed a labyrinth far beneath my feet, and I began to wonder how the humans found their way without finding themselves lost.

The number of humans I could plainly see was frightening. They were everywhere, coming out of every corner of this labyrinth like termites crawling in and around their mound...hundreds and hundreds of them... more than I could possibly count. And what's more, their children were everywhere at all stages of development, as if the humans reproduced at an alarming rate.

Fear began to burn in my heart--not the natural fear of being found by this swarm of humans, but a gut-wrenching fear for the rest of the lands. How long would it take for them to reach Rhodarion? Aleodyn? All of Akelian?

Without another thought, I grabbed my rope and plummeted toward the ground with extreme haste. The rest of the elves had to know about this--and I had to tell them.

Aleodyn was the closest kingdom, and Telenor was the high priest at the time. He had always been good to me, so I set out for the forest high upon the cliff-side.

After a swift journey, I finally walked through the twin willows that marked the entrance of the Aleodyn castle. In the massive throne room full of elves of every kingdom, my good friend Telenor sat upon his throne alongside his wife, an elf of staggering beauty. She had the fiery red hair and emerald green eyes of her people, but her perfectly almond shaped eyes, rosy cheeks and innocent smile, gave her a beauty far beyond her subjects.

I knelt before her grace and beauty as I gave word of my discovery, and of the humans.

"Destroyed? The western lands?" the beautiful priestess asked from her throne.

"Yes, my lady Viridae," I replied, rising to my feet with a heavy heart. "And the humans have achieved great numbers in a very short period of time. This pride seems to have more humans than we have elves in all of our kingdoms combined."

Viridae remained seated and silent, digesting the information and exchanging a serious expression with her husband, an elf of great kindness and honor who was stroking his long red beard thoughtfully. But time seemed of the essence. Did we really have time so sit and mull over the actions of these creatures? Every moment spent in silence was another moment for the humans to spread their destruction.

I called out forcefully to the high priest and priestess. Perhaps I did not have the right or authority to do so, but to sit idly seemed foolish.

"My lord and lady, these humans are dangerous. They will destroy all of Akelian, leaving nothing and no one in their wake if we do not try to stop them."

Lady Viridae stared right into my eyes, examining my expression and urgency.

"The red light shows strongly in your words, Amphor," she said through a silvery voice with a kind smile. "War or battle is not the solution here, my friend. To take our elves to war is to lead them to certain death, and we alone stand to protect nature and this great earth. Who would remain if we all perished in senseless battle?"

***

"Hold on," Darion interrupted, and Demetri was sure he was bubbling with the same thought. *"Amphor?"*

With a melancholy expression, she closed the book slightly and looked at them, still holding her finger where they left off.

"Yes. Amphor," she said as a faint smile spread across her face, a smile that was clearly being faked.

"Like Amphy? Is that the guy Amphy was named after?" Demetri pried excitedly--but Gema didn't respond right away, seemingly lost in deep thought.

"I found the name in this book, boys," she finally said in a quiet voice. "When you brought home a fox, Dare, this was the first name that came to me. That's why I suggested it to you. Amphor is a red light, and Amphy was full of fire. It just seemed to fit."

"Amphor *is?*" Darion asked, wide eyed. "So he's still alive today?"

"Was," Gema corrected herself. "Forgive my mistake. Shall we continue?"

***

I could think of nothing to say as I stood there, feeling slightly foolish. I was right to be worried about the future demise of our world, but at the same time, I could not ignore the sense and wisdom behind her silvery words.

Telenor stood from his throne, addressing all that were in the throne room on that day--every sage, every guard, and every subject present.

"Lady Viridae is right," he announced with an echoing voice. "We cannot achieve victory in battle, and it is not our place to destroy those that we do not understand. We shall live, and let live..."

All I could do was stare, anger and frustration rising like a mighty flame in my chest. Why would they not take this seriously?

"...Yet we will not sit idly," Telenor added, and I felt my fiery rage die down... but the embers still burned red hot. Turning to face the other elves in the throne room, he addressed them in a commanding, deep voice.

"Set up guards around every kingdom, and do not let the humans enter our sacred lands. One elf from each kingdom will act as a messenger, and you will send word to the other kingdoms. Five of you--" he walked among his sages positioned just to the side of his throne, touching five of them on the shoulders as he passed, "--will go in search of the three white lights. As you know, they wander between the four kingdoms to maintain harmony. No white lights are currently in Aleodyn, so search the other three kingdoms. The rest of our Aleodyn sages will form a watch party and return to the human kingdom. Try to gather as much information as possible, but keep out of sight. Determining if they have any other prides in the land is your top priority. We need to know how many of them are out there and the extent of their damage."

Telenor returned to his throne in silence, where he sat with his head held high.

"When you feel that you have gathered as much information as you can, return here."

All of the sages saluted and bowed in unison, but I stood there, unsure of my next

move. Should I return to my own kingdom
as a messenger, sounding the alarm and
helping them to prepare?

"Amphor," Viridae's silver voice called
out, and I turned to look at her. "We have a
messenger for your kingdom, so fear not. I
would like you to go with our sages, to help
them find this human pride quickly and
carefully."

My heart bounded with determination as
I nodded my head and bowed, my mission
having been given to me--a mission for
which I was thankful. My guidance was of
much more use than my ability to deliver a
message.

Finding the humans again was simple.
Finding information about them was much
more challenging. We could not risk the
humans finding out about us before our
mission was complete, so we proceeded with
great caution--caution which made gathering
information an arduous task.

Sages were stationed in many places
around the forest, and one could not ask for
a better fleet of lookouts than the Aleodyn
court of sages. Their eyesight was a mighty

wonder in Akelian, and they could scope out the landscape many miles ahead of them with great ease, allowing them to see but never be seen. Even the eagles were envious.

As they surveyed from high in the trees, I remained on the ground, stealthily gathering information from as close to the humans as I could get without detection.

Many months passed, months of endless watching and waiting. It seemed that the humans had only two major settlements, a kingdom in the northern mountains being their second one. This kingdom seemed to be smaller than the first one, but at least one hundred humans still called this kingdom home.

During my watch of this smaller kingdom, I noticed something that sparked my attention. The humans had destroyed the natural land in this area as well, but the kingdom didn't seem to be spreading any further...

After a while, I began to think of the human monsters a bit differently. It seemed that they were not trying to consume all of the lands after all, only the land that they needed. Perhaps these creatures were not cold and heartless as I had thought before... perhaps they were just unaware of how important it was to live in harmony with nature.

They weren't monsters--they were ignorant.

Upon this startling realization, I gathered my fellow watchers and told them to prepare to return to Aleodyn. This was the information the High Priest and Priestess needed most of all.

The first thing I noticed, when I entered the grand throne room, were three more thrones sitting alongside the thrones of Telenor and Viridae...and what beautiful thrones they were. White, petrified wood had been intricately carved into strands of vines inter-weaved together, lined with strands of silver and giving off brilliant shine, like stars that had fallen to earth and landed on these ethereal thrones.

Yet the brilliance and beauty of these thrones were nothing compared to the elves that sat in them, and I could not help but gape openly, captivated by their beauty. All three had long, platinum hair that fell in straight lines, like cascading silk framing their fair-skinned faces and mesmerizing turquoise eyes. Elegant, flowing white robes hung from their shoulders, enhancing their pure glow.

As soon I laid eyes on them I knew--the three white lights had been found, and here they sat among the court of Aleodyn. I was nearly blinded by their beauty, and their pure spirits flooded the room with a strange tingling energy, a blissful feeling of peace and harmony. Two males, Eredir and Alberen, and the lady Miradel--the only female white light alive.

"You bring news, brave Amphor?" said Viridae, jarring me out of my stupor.

"Yes, my lady...The humans seem to be unaware of the damage they cause," I said truthfully. "And I believe that they need to be educated rather than eradicated."

Miradel's beautiful face positively beamed at my words, and her radiant glow filled me with pure joy and bliss...Lady Miradel had just smiled at my idea...

"A very wise observation, Amphor," she chimed in an echoing angelic voice. I felt my blood flush my face, and I hoped that the white lights wouldn't see this mighty warrior blush.

The Lady Miradel rose from her seat with such flowing grace that she resembled a ghost, floating effortlessly through the room. Her sweet voice, like the chiming of bells, echoed throughout the entire throne room as she spoke, though she spoke in calm, dulcet tones.

"Take the sages and extend to the humans an offer of peace. We will walk with them and teach them the ways of nature. Offer our wisdom and grace, for it is the wisdom and grace of the earth. It belongs to everyone, not the elves alone."

She turned to me, her turquoise eyes peering into my very soul.

"Young Amphor," she chimed, "there is no one better for the task that I appoint to you. You, and you alone, must approach the leader of the humans. Do not fear your short fuse and fiery disposition--" It was as if my eyes were a book and my thoughts

were the words etched onto the pages,
and she was reading every line. Every
fear and vulnerability that I tucked far
into the corners of my mind were there,
and she knew just which pages to turn to.
Yet somehow, this was a comforting and
welcome thought, and she smiled graciously
as her angelic voice washed over me, giving
me comfort with every word she spoke. "--for
I can see that you are truly the only one who
can do this the way it needs to be done, with
grace and compassion."

Her hands wrapped around a small chain
around her neck, and she carefully pulled it
over her head, revealing an elegant pendant
of silver and pearl that had been tucked
into her robes. With a smooth and gentle
touch, she grabbed my calloused hand and
placed the pendant in it, closing my fingers
around it.

"Take this with you. When you wear it,
you will find yourself connected to every
human you meet on a spiritual level. You
will be able to understand their language,
and they will find themselves able to
understand you. As you accept this pendant,

you accept this mission of dire importance, and you accept your role as Captain."

Such beautiful words of wisdom I would never forget. I could think of nothing to say that wouldn't pale in comparison to them, so I simply bowed my head and accepted my mission, bursting with pride.

Together with my party of Sages, we headed out toward the kingdom of the humans. Our thoughts drifted warmly to the thought of the white lights, and of Lady Miradel, and blissful light and peace followed our every step.

With my head held high and Lady Miradel's soothing words in my heart, I approached the door of the great gray gate, the same one that I had scaled so many months ago. Nearly as tall as the stone wall itself and towering far above my head, this door seemed to be the only entrance to the kingdom. I waited in anticipation.

To my surprise and relief, the gate opened slowly, revealing cold stone streets eerily winding their way like gray snakes through the stone houses.

As I strutted purposefully through the
flat streets headed for the enormous castle
in the distance, I saw humans staring at me
from nearly every window. I held my head
high, but even at my full height, the top of
my head barely reached their chests. Most
had stares of venom and fear, but a precious
few smiled at me as I passed--most of them
children.

After arduously navigating to the center
of the Labyrinth, I found myself standing in
front of the imposing castle doors...

Hesitation won't bring peace, I thought
to myself as I stared at the doors, a nervous
prickle in my stomach. Closing my hand
around Lady Miradel's pendant hanging
close to my heart, I took a deep breath and
opened the door.

Sitting on a plush throne in the middle
of the great room was a toweringly tall
human with a long brown beard and a sharp
look in his eyes. I approached the man with
trepidation, respectfully bowing to the leader
of the humans and hoping that this gesture
would translate in their culture.

To my immediate relief, it did. He bowed to me with a welcoming but curious smile. In that moment, the sheer immensity of this moment and what I was trying to accomplish hit me hard, and it took every ounce of determination to do what I needed to do next...speak to him.

"I wish to extend greetings from the kingdoms of elves, for this is a momentous occasion. Our two races have finally met, and we wish to offer friendship and peace with our newfound kin. Forgive me," I said as I bowed low once again. "...but my kind was unsure what name belonged to your mighty race, so we have dubbed you 'humans'. We hope that this pleases you."

To my surprise, the human rose from his seat and walked toward me, not aggressively, but with a certain delight in his step. He held out his hand and I took it. For some reason, he shook my hand up and down and laughed gleefully. "We only ever called ourselves beings, but I like the name 'human' better. So I suppose we are now 'human beings'?"

I smiled in return, grateful for Lady Miradel's pendant, and our ability to understand each other and speak freely.

"I am called Borowan," he informed me kindly, "and I am the King of this land. The kingdom itself is called Bellumor."

So many questions about these giants were forming in my mind, and I couldn't help but be taken aback by the kindness of the King.

"The leader of the humans is called a 'King'?" I asked, unable to mask my curiosity.

"Why, yes," King Borowan answered, chuckling slightly. "And what title belongs to the leader of the elves?"

"We refer to our leaders as High Priests and Priestesses," I offered, ready to share with this kind stranger. "There is a Priest and Priestess for each of our Kingdoms, which are Mer Anemos in the southeast, Solaurhia in the east, Aleodyn in the north, and my kingdom, Rhodarion, in the south. Each kingdom also has a court of sages as well, a group of elves sworn to protect the Priests and the kingdom."

"Yes, yes," he said, nodding his head. "Sages are called 'knights' in my kingdom. My knights are the ones that protect my subjects and me. What is your name, good sir?"

"Amphor," I answered. "Amphor of Rhodarion."

"Well then, Amphor of Rhodarion, would you do the the honor of walking with me through the royal gardens? I am most anxious to hear more of your kind."

It must have looked strange to any human beings looking on as we walked through the gardens. The great King lightly ambling around with a man the size of their children, sharing delightful stories and fascinating traditions as equals. I walked with Borowan for hours that day, taking in fascinating tales of his kind--and his equal fascination with my world made my chest swell with delight.

This may have been important historical meeting with a serious purpose, but King Borowan was an absolute joy to be around. He told me about his kingdoms, both Bellumor and Evanesca, the kingdom we had been watching in the mountains. The humans believed that natural elements existed to serve their kind and aid in their survival. The thought that nature had its own beauty and important balance had never even entered their minds. As he told me this, I felt my heart fall into the pit of my stomach. How could such a good, kind man be so horribly wrong?

I continued to walk with him, patiently telling him of the elvish ways--to love nature and live in harmony with its great flowing spirit. As I explained, I could see the confusion in his eyes. *Our ways must seem silly to him*, I remember thinking to myself at the time. If they believed that nature was just a great resource at their disposal, learning to live in harmonic existence with your resources would seem a laughable matter.

Just as I began to fear that no compromise on our beliefs could be made, King Borowan offered a proposal. The humans would not expand their kingdoms any further, and would respect the natural land outside of their borders. The elves would leave the humans to live their own lives within their borders, no matter how harmful it was to the land within those borders. As long as the humans were mindful of nature outside of their own borders and the elves let the humans be, peace could exist between the two races.

Though I hated the thought of any natural land being destroyed, I knew that this sacrifice would ensure the safety of the elvish kingdoms, and all of Akelian--so I agreed.

Back in the throne room, Borowan and I took an oath of peace, signing a treaty that we thought would exist for all time. In that moment, I bade my new friend farewell to inform the rest of my people--we finally had the promise of peace.

***

The Fall of Evanesca

"Gema...this is all real, right?" Demetri asked with hesitation. "I mean, that peace treaty really happened...right?"

"Yes," Gema said, rocking slightly in her rocking chair, "Amphor was a great hero that day, bringing peace to the land for many decades."

"I'm sensing a 'but' in there somewhere," Darion interjected as the wind blew his sandy blond hair into his blue eyes. He brushed it back out of his face as Demetri turned to look at Gema. Staring at them with deep sadness, she didn't say a word.

She simply looked back down at the book, picking up where she had left off.

***

Many decades had passed since the dawn of the peace treaty, and I had spent many long days in the company of King Borowan, who quickly became a dear friend. I learned many things about his kind in my time with him--the most troubling of which I had to find out on my own--in the most cruel way.

Merely forty short years after my first meeting with the King, a human messenger appeared in my Kingdom, carrying a solemn face and a message of despair--the King lay dying, his young son about to take over the throne...and he wished to see me one last time.

With the swiftness of an eagle, I dashed toward Bellumor and this terrible tragedy. Borowan was so young after all, only seventy years old. My heart bled for him, for his kingdom, and for his young son, Borin. How frightening it must be to have to take on the throne at only twenty-two years old...just a child...

I finally found my way to the castle and prepared to enter the throne room, but a knight bade me to follow him to the King's bed chamber. The dark shadow of death hung heavily over the chamber as I entered, Borowan lying on a lavish bed with a post on every corner, where crimson curtains hung to shield him from unwanted eyes. Save two guards at the door, only his son was present in the cavernous room, wearing a melancholy look upon his young face. With great care, I approached the lavish bed and slowly pulled the crimson curtains away.

Deep lines were etched into his pale face, green with sickness, his chest rising ever so slightly as he breathed shallow, painful breaths...

My heart couldn't take it. A sharp ache pierced through my chest into every corner of my soul, and I couldn't stop the tears from welling up in my eyes. It felt as though something had a hold on my heart and was squeezing as hard as it could...it was death.

Death had taken hold of my heart, as it took hold of my friend's life.

Borowan slowly opened his eyes and they met mine, though I could barely see through the veil of my tears.

"My old friend," he croaked, faintly smiling as he held out his hand. I took it into mine, the tears finally trickling down my cheeks.

"Amphor, I lie here awaiting death to take me to the great beyond," he whispered weakly. "As I wait ever so patiently, memories flood my mind to keep me company...and the memories that give me the most comfort--well, they are the ones of you..." He smiled faintly as he fell silent for a moment, catching his breath. I sat on the edge of his grand bed, still holding his frail hand in mine as he gave a weak chuckle.

"You haven't aged a single day since we met, you fortunate creature... I fall victim to the never ending cycle of age and time..."

Borin stood over his father on the other side of the bed, and as I looked up in that moment, he stared at me with deep suspicion. I leaned over, my lips as close to Borowan's ears as I could get, and I whispered words of comfort to my dear friend--words that only he could hear.

"Never fear, my friend. Our time together is not at an end... this is merely a pause. For I too will join you one day, on the other side of death. We will wander the great beyond together for all eternity, sharing stories and laughing once again--Borowan?"

As I looked into my friend's unseeing eyes, I breathed a sorrowful breath and let the tears flow freely for the first time in my life. The mighty king of Bellumor and Evanesca--the founder of peace between elves and men--stared into nothing and breathed no more...the faint smile from my farewell words still on his face.

Death squeezed my heart with such force; I found it hard to breathe, to take in such devastation. All I craved in that moment was solitude.

I laid my hand on Borowan's face and gently closed his eyes, then turned toward the door with a heavy heart.

"Why?" shouted the Dark haired Borin, halting my steps. I respectfully turned to

face the new King--he had inherited his
father's sharp eyes.

"Why has age shown you so much mercy?
My father knew you for nearly 40 years, and
you still have the face of someone my age."
Venom laced his every word. "Where do you
get such powerful longevity?"

I had no words of comfort for this grieving
son full of misplaced bitterness, so I simply
bowed my head and turned back toward the
door.

"I know of your sacred cave," he yelled
quickly. I stopped just before the door, but
this time I refused to turn around.

"The Cave of Erathae," he continued. "Is
that the answer? Some sort of sacred cave
of youth?" Rage shook his booming voice.
"Could you have even saved my father?!"

In that moment, that tense, tragic
moment, one of my fears had come to
life. There are few greater powers in this
world than the love between a father and
son-- combine that intense love with loss
and rage, and people will fall into darkness
before your very eyes.

I said nothing as I left the room, a sense of dread mingled with the painful ache in my heart. Perhaps this was my mistake, simply walking away without a thought of calming this raging child--and I have spent many long nights wondering how different things would be today if I had just stayed a few moments longer, taking the time to try to reason with this grief stricken child--no longer a child, but a newly-crowned man with great power...

The rage of King Borin, so young to lose so much, echoed far throughout Akelian. His resentment toward me evolved into hatred--as I was informed shortly after returning to my home--and the hate did not end there.

Not too long after Borowan's death, elves were no longer welcome in the kingdoms of men, and for an elf to show his face in the human realms, the penalty was death--a cruel, merciless death on sight.

***

"What a brat," Demetri blurted out, folding his arms. "I mean seriously, who blames someone completely unrelated for someone else's death? Amphor wasn't even there until right before he died!"

"Grief can make people do strange things, Demetri," Gema said softly. He felt his jaw drop, feeling like he had just gotten slapped in the face--Gema never called him Demetri...

"Suddenly," she continued in a soft, melancholic voice, "your whole world turns upside down when you lose someone that close to you. Nothing makes sense to you, and you just can't understand how the world works anymore. You try desperately to find a reason behind your loss, but you never come up with anything at all, and it drives you mad. With no answers, some people make up their own answers to try to find that closure--and that's what poor Borin did. In his mind, Amphor being responsible for his father's death, by holding onto precious secrets of immortality, gave him the answer to that burning question that haunts all who have lost a loved one: *why?* And now he had his answer, no matter how wrong it was."

She sighed deeply before continuing. "Have pity on the grieving, my grandsons. Even if you have felt the pain of losing someone close to you, as I know you have--" she glanced meaningfully at Darion. "--you will never truly know what another grieving person is feeling, or how badly they are hurting. Please, always hold onto your empathy...do you know what that means?"

They both shook their heads.

"Empathy means to put yourself in another person's shoes, to be able to look at life from that person's point of view, and understand why they do the things that they do. Empathy is the absolute most important key to peace and harmony in this world. If you can't feel what another feels, you can never truly understand. And understanding leads to compassion, and care...and then to peace. Without empathy, there can be no harmony."

The boys exchanged uncomfortable looks before staring back at her. Darion seemed just as unsure about all of this as Demetri felt.

"I know this is a long story. Would you boys like to take a break? It is your birthday after all."

"No," said Darion quickly.

Both Gema and Demetri looked at him in shock. Darion wanted to hear *more* of an elvish tale?

"You said this would tell us why we had to leave Bellumor," he said seriously, "and I want to know."

Gema nodded her head in understanding, and looked down at the book once again.

***

Every elvish kingdom was placed on high alert--Guards took their places along the borders; defenses were put into place--I watched the evolution of our great land, a land once full of peace, now full of fear and pain...and misdirected rage. I longed for the days of old, where men and elves could pass through each other's lands with joy and serenity, learning each other's ways and making trade, bettering the lives of one another...

My heart wept for my world.

Then, the unthinkable happened.

It was quite by chance that I was in Aleodyn when it did. I had simply been craving the company of a good friend since Borowan's death, so I had sought out High Priest Telenor. Sitting among the ferns of his forest, voicing our concerns of this new world, we were jolted out of our conversation when a messenger darted toward us, panting heavily as he tried to speak.

"My Priest...humans...hundreds... weapons...headed this way..."

Telenor and I didn't wait to for him to catch his breath. Dashing through the forest at top speed, we headed straight for the tree-lined throne room.

Gasps went around the room as Telenor gave this grave news. Viridae held her hand up to her beautiful mouth in shock.

"But why?" she asked. "Surely there is nothing to be gained by simply destroying our people or our lands?"

"I know not, my dear," Telenor said gently. "I do not believe anyone knows what exactly they are after."

My stomach plummeted as a memory flooded my mind--the memory of the last time I laid eyes on Borin--

"I may, my lady," I said woefully, and she stared at me curiously through her vivid green eyes.

"Please tell us," she said. Though she radiated strength and wisdom, her voice trembled slightly. "You were close to King Borowan--tell us all you know."

"Erathae...It's the Cave of Erathae. When last I spoke with Borin, he spoke of the cave as if it were a cave of youth. I believe he thinks it has the power to fight mortality."

Viridae nervously ran her hand through her fiery red hair, and Telenor placed his hand gently on her shoulder. For a while, all sound was silenced by the intense fear smothering the room.

"Then we have no time to lose," Telenor finally concluded. "We must gather all of our forces and make for the cave...the elves must prepare for war."

The words cut like knives, straight to the core of everyone in the throne room. The Priests of every other elvish kingdom entered hastily through the hall of kingdoms, a magnificent place of magic that connected all of the High priest's castles in a single grand hall, a short cut that allowed the leaders of our world to communicate freely without worry of the vast distance between kingdoms--a place worth every speck of its magic on a day like this.

Our great leaders began preparations, ready to fight. Priests and sages alike huddled together, muttering plans and strategies...a bizarre right to behold. War was a cold and dreary time that elves had never faced before.

The sages of all kingdoms prepared for the inevitable war at the mouth of Erathae, but with little hope. Evanesca was much closer to Erathae than any of the kingdoms, and even if we moved with lightning speed, there was still the chance that they would get there first. The humans could also easily overwhelm us with sheer numbers--this was a fight we could not win.

***

Though he dared not interrupt Gema, Demetri noticed a change in the handwriting in the book once again. It looked like the same handwriting as the previous passage, but much more shaky and scratchy. It was as if Amphor had to learn how to write all over again.

***

It has been a precious long time since I have been able to write, and I'm lucky to be writing at all. I'm lucky to be breathing. Powerful visions flood my body...memories... such horrible memories...They repeat in my head over and over again without end--I'm beginning to think I'm going mad...

Perhaps writing about such horrible memories will get them onto the paper and out of my mind, though no amount of writing could ever take away what I have seen.

King Borin sent an army after the sacred cave, and we had no choice but to fight. We had no choice...that's what I keep telling myself...

By a sheer stroke of luck, Erathae remained hidden from the humans when our tiny band of elves arrived, all clad in swords and bows, shields and daggers. Under the cover of nightfall, our warriors stood in front of Erathae, watching...waiting.

I helped arrange Rhodarion sages on the front lines. No elf wants to be a warrior, but if a warrior is needed, no elf is better for the job than a fiery red light. Solaurhian sages joined my elves on the front lines, leaning on their expert sword skills and their magnificent shields, full of lethal light beams harvested from the afternoon sun and stored in the shields themselves, ready to be unleashed onto the enemy. Mer Anemos sages had set up traps for miles around the cave, and then returned to fight. The keen eyesight and impeccable archery skills of the Aleodyn sages were both greatly needed, and they perched themselves high in the treetops.

Something rustled through the forest under the cover of the night, footsteps... marching closer...closer...

I could hear the faint scraping of arrows being taken out of quills, the soft sing of swords being unsheathed. My heart hammered in my chest, threatening to burst out and join the battle on its own. All of our sages seemed to be holding their breath, afraid to make even a faint sound.

Closer...closer...

The blue light sages closed their eyes and waved their hands in front of them in a fluid motion--the very air around us seemed to thicken. Within mere seconds, we were shrouded in a dense fog, shielding us from all without elvish eyes.

Closer...closer...

Palms sweating, hands trembling, my very breath seemed stolen away from me. Shocked screams pierced the air along with the sound of swiftly moving ropes.

"The traps are working," Telenor whispered from the trees above me.

Something whizzed through my raven hair, and I turned to see an arrow embedded in the tree just behind me...

Roaring screams sounded in every direction. We were surrounded.

"FIRE!!" Telenor screamed with ferocity. Arrows flew through the sky like shooting stars, flying right past the elves and into the human ranks--every single one of them found their mark.

"Yes!" I roared, pumping my fist in the air--but the sound of more charging humans put a stop to my early celebration.

"FIRE!!" Telenor shouted again, a note of panic in his voice. Blood curdling screams told me that the humans had fallen again... but still more came...Telenor looked down at me--panic threatened to take me as well--we were all shaking in our skin--

Everything around me seemed to fade out, as if sound had suddenly dissolved out of existence. Time itself seemed to have slowed down. The pure horror of what was in front of me seemed impossible for my brain to process.

I looked around.

My men--my brothers--were trembling with fear and stumbling backward. These humans, horribly violent and confused creatures, were going to set foot in our most beautiful, most sacred lands--and rip them apart. All for fear of death...for a longer life. My brothers were going to be slaughtered, the wise and strong leaders of nature and harmony--every flower and every tree, every mouse and every deer, every mountain and every river...all gruesomely ripped to shreds and powdered into dust...

My blood was ice cold from fear only seconds ago, but in that moment, I burned as it boiled.

No more, I thought to myself. Shouting in righteous anger, I stood before my quaking men.

"You are servants of the great spirit of nature! You were shaped into unbeatable weapons by the earth itself! You are the only hope that this good land has! Stand your ground! Fight for nature! Fight for life!"

I wasn't even thinking as I ran through the fog, roaring at the top of my lungs, toward the humans. As I look back on that moment full of rage and terror, it was almost certain suicide. But as I charged forward, the roar of one hundred charging elves came from right beside me--

Arrows flew and swords slashed haphazardly through the mist. The humans may have been many, but they were blind. I dashed through the onslaught of helpless humans as sages struck them to the ground.

Blue lights gathered water from the air and froze them into ice daggers that sliced through the air around me. Branches whipped around on the trees, slashing and binding our enemies. There may have been no sun, but the yellow sages did not sit idle. Beams of sun rays shot through the darkness in bursts, burning the humans to ash in mere seconds. Swords and daggers expertly wielded sliced through flesh--blood splattered the shadowed grass.

But me? My fire was reserved for one and one only. I would take the life of one to spare the lives of many--but as I charged through the death and destruction all around me, I found that Telenor had gotten there first--

With swords clanging, flashes of Telenor's red beard streaked through the air as he nimbly dodged the slashing blade of King Borin, who was baring his teeth in a hideous snarl. As swift as a hummingbird's wing, Borin's sword wielding proved to be terrifying and unequaled...

With fire raging in my chest, I charged toward them, a white-hot fireball growing quickly in my palm.

Hearing my charge, Telenor turned his head toward me, away from the fight for just a second--

Borin seized his shoulder--shoved a dagger through his chest--

The world seemed to melt from underneath me as I froze in place, watching as my dear friend fell in slow motion to the ground... the shock of his last mistake still on his face...

I roared with a burning, fiery rage. Nothing else in the world existed anymore. It was just me, and the monster who murdered my friend.

I charged with blinding ferocity, my teeth bared. Borin sharply pulled the dagger from Telenor's chest and turned to face me, Telenor's blood oozing down the blade onto his hand. With such swift swordplay, building a fireball in my hand was simply out of the question. He slashed, and I slid, aiming for the sword lying at Telenor's side...

The hilt met my hand and I shot up, holding my friend's sword in front of my face just in time to save it from Borin's powerful slash--the clanging from our mighty clashing swords rang through the air--Borin moved with lightning speed and expert agility. As I slowed from exhaustion, his strokes kept coming--his energy seemed infinite--faster and faster--I couldn't keep up--

It happened so fast that it was over before it began. With two effortless slashes and a flash of searing pain, I hit the ground bleeding freely--my arm and leg parted from my body...

As I lay there, consciousness threatening to elude me, I stared in horror at the carnage before me...Men and elves were lying everywhere now, drenched in blood, eyes glossed over...never to see again. Precious children were now fatherless. Families built out of love were now torn apart by senseless hate--

Raindrops pattered the ground, and a very familiar feeling prickled in my stomach as the world started fading...the feeling that...all hope was lost...that we never even stood a chance...

The fuzzy silhouette of Borin appeared in front of my eyes, and he barked a menacing laugh as he stood over my bleeding body, still wielding the dagger that claimed Telenor's life.

Then, his laughter abruptly stopped--he charged straight for me.

Whether it was instinct or skill, I still cannot say for sure. But somehow, I twisted my mangled body out of the way, tearing the dagger away from him with my one hand and plunging it straight into his back.

As I dizzily panted, King Borin of Bellumor, son of the Good King Borowan, fell to his knees and dropped, face first, onto the ground right beside me, and breathed his last breath of hatred.

Now I could die in peace...

A bright light came from the summit of the mountains, nearly blinding me as I lay there gasping for breath--death was finally coming for me--

But was this truly death? Searing pain still shot throughout my body, and surely pain did not carry on after death...

The brilliant light slowly dimmed, revealing three stunning figures with turquoise eyes riding on the backs of massive snow leopards. As they flew past me, my bleeding stumps tingled wildly and the pain dissolved. I looked down to see myself still sitting in a pool of my own blood, arm and leg still severed, but my injuries were healed.

They reached the center of battle and dismounted, a hauntingly angry look in their eyes. I looked upon the humans as they laid down their arms--gaping in wonder--their weak hearts flooded by the radiating beauty that stood before them, a beauty far beyond anything they had ever seen, or could ever comprehend.

Miradel was the first to speak. Though she never shouted, her angelic voice was eerie and haunting--and terrifying.

"Your king is defeated, and you have no hope of defeating us. The battle is won." Her voice echoed through the air like shimmering bells in a silent graveyard.

She had a kind but eerie expression on her beautiful face, and all stared at her in terrified awe as she walked, completely unarmed but fearless, among the human ranks.

"We have taken many more of your kind than we ever wished to. Surrender now and we will heal your injured. Return to Bellumor, but leave Evanesca to the mountains...let the land recover from your carnage."

Her beautiful turquoise eyes suddenly flashed from kindness to haunting severity.

"If you do not surrender, we will destroy all who remain."

Never before had such a small, angelic creature caused so much fear--every surviving human knelt before the three white lights. Miradel and the two males walked among the injured, healing every single human as promised. The quaking soldiers bowed to them once again before turning to flee the mountains, never to return.

We may have won the battle, but the horror I saw that fateful night would stay with me for the rest of my life. For anger to lead to so much bloodshed...to see the blood of my brothers pooling in the grass, bodies twitching and howling...begging...praying...It haunts my dreams to this very day.

I lead Rhodarion as High Priest now, and I lead with the frail hope of peace. The humans remain a suppressed threat to our lands and our people, but I vow that my kingdom will not be the first to strike. With every passing day I prepare for war, while praying for peace.

***

Staring at the final page with glistening eyes, Gema slowly closed the book and looked up at the boys.

"That war...was real?" Darion stuttered. "People really died?"

"Hundreds died that day, Darion. Hundreds upon hundreds. But the tragedy doesn't stop there," she said heavily. "Can you imagine how much pain flooded this earth with the lost lives of those men? Wives were left to raise their children alone, children that would grow up never knowing what it meant to be loved by a father. The affects of war do not stop when the battles are over. They loom on in this world for generations to come, through the tainted souls of the ones left to survive."

"What happened next?" asked Demetri cautiously, and Gema leaned back in her rocking chair, letting her long hair fall through the back of it onto the floor.

"Well, since the cave of Erathae wasn't safe anymore, the elves decided to hide it and make it to where no human even stood a chance of finding it. That's how Lumaneire was born--The Great White Kingdom as it's known to humans. There is no place in Akelian that is better protected."

Demetri couldn't stop himself. "Where is it?" he blurted out excitedly.

Gema chuckled softly at his enthusiasm, though her face remained etched with melancholy. "Nowhere. At least, not anymore."

Demetri's heart sank, but Darion stared at her in disbelief.

"How on earth can a kingdom be *nowhere?*" he asked.

"It's gone, but not gone. It's here in Akelian, but nowhere to be found. Lumaneire is a magical kingdom that only appears when the elves are in need--it never appears for long, and is never found in the same place twice."

Something clicked in Demetri's mind. "So *that's* why I wouldn't be able to find the cave of Erathae!"

"Yes," Gema confirmed.

Demetri looked at Darion with his mouth hanging open in awe, but Darion seemed unsatisfied.

"What happened to Bellumor? I get that there was a war who knows how long ago, but why did that mean we had to leave?" Bitter resentment rang in his voice, and Demetri glanced at the pendant engraved with the symbol of Bellumor still hanging from his brother's neck.

"Two different questions with two completely different answers," said Gema as she rocked gently in her chair. "After Borin was defeated, a knight by the name of Taremus was given the throne. He was next in line because he was of royal blood, you see. He was Borin's younger cousin. But even though he shared the same blood as Borin, he didn't share his beliefs. Much to the dismay of the rest of the humans, King Taremus sought to bring back the peace treaty, and Miradel herself left the safety of Lumaneire to sign it."

"So...why exactly did we have to leave?" Darion asked again. Gema sighed heavily.

"Because the humans don't want that peace treaty, Darion. Don't you understand? The elves killed hundreds of humans that day--decimated hundreds of families. Everyone in those families grew to hate the elves that took their loved ones away."

"But they were just defending themselves," Demetri mumbled.

"You're absolutely right, Tree. The elves were merely doing what they had to do to protect themselves and the land," Gema agreed, nodding her head slightly. "But if you tried telling that to the children who lost their fathers, or the wives that lost their husbands, they would slam the door in your face. Do you remember what I said about losing a loved one? The question '*why*'? The humans desperately needed an answer to that question--so they crafted one for themselves. Elves--that's why. The stench of hatred still looms over the lands to this day."

She looked through the front window into the house, and Demetri turned to see Mom busily tidying up and Dad lacing up his shoes.

"The humans refuse to see the truth behind their loss," Gema continued, "but the Anbidian family...we've always known the truth-- and *that's* why we had to leave. Our support of the elves in such a hateful society could have cost us our lives. Many of our neighbors spat on our doors, believing us to be traitors. You boys didn't deserve that, being shunned in every corner of your home. We came to the forest to live a good life, free from persecution."

"And there's nothing we can do?" Darion asked woefully, and to Demetri's surprise, Gema smiled at him.

"Be the very best you can be," she said gently. "With every passing day, remember to be good and kind, compassionate and caring, and above all, understanding. Respect all living things, great or small, and always help someone in need--but above all, never, ever, forget the greatest weapon for peace--empathy. Carry it with you everywhere, and use it always."

"But...how will that help stop such a big war?" Demetri asked, disappointed. It felt like they were waist deep in water on a sinking ship, and Gema just handed them a spoon.

She laughed through a sigh in her voice. "That is the *only* thing that can stop such a big war."

All Demetri could do was sit there, trying to make sense of her words. Part of him felt like it was just another silly Gema notion... but part of him felt like he truly understood.

"Now then," she said, going from melancholy whisper to her usual, light hearted voice. "I told you both yesterday to

think about what you want from your old
Gema for your birthday. What did you come
up with?"

"Oh I'm good actually," said Darion
vaguely as Gema looked to him. "I was
actually going to ask you to tell me about
Bellumor--but I've heard enough. I don't
need or hear any more."

As she turned to Demetri, he remembered
his frustration from earlier that morning,
sleeplessly thinking about what exactly he
wanted...coming up with nothing...

"I just want an *adventure,* Gema,"
he finally whispered, feeling slightly
embarrassed. "That's all I really want
this year... I know it's silly, but it's all I
really want...but I know you can't give me
something like that."

"Oh, maybe not," she said with a
mischievous grin. "But perhaps I can give
you a place to begin one."

"...Huh?" Demetri said, feeling completely
lost.

But at that moment, the front door
creaked open and Dad leaned his head
through.

"Boys, get your shoes on. I want you to come with me. Are they ready, Mom?"

"Yes son," she said confidently. "Now they're ready."

Demetri's eyes were alight with joy as he shot up from his stool, unable to contain his excitement. He kissed Gema on the cheek and then politely pushed past Dad to put on his shoes, which were just on the other side of the front door. As he sat there lacing them up, he could hear Darion's voice through the open door...

"Thanks," he said, and Demetri could hear genuine gratitude in his voice.

"For what, dear?" Gema asked as the rocking chair continued to creak.

"...For telling us."

Even though Demetri couldn't see her face, he was sure she was smiling. He had to admit, things felt much different now that he knew why they were out here in the middle of nowhere--the world seemed like a much different, much more dangerous place...

Once they were in the woods with Dad, it took them no time at all to realize where they were going. They had traveled down this trail all summer, after all...

"Hey Dad!" Darion called out from somewhere behind Demetri as he crunched through the fallen leaves on the ground. "I thought you said we couldn't come out here because of the wolves!"

--He had a good point. Demetri certainly didn't think getting gobbled up by a wolf was an appropriate way to spend your twelfth birthday.

"Oh yeah--that was a clever lie wasn't it?" Dad beamed with a toothy grin, obviously very pleased with himself, but as they approached the hideout clearing they could hardly understand why. A tangled mess of autumn seemed to have overtaken their beautiful meadow with their hideout. Bushes just seemed to have grown on top of each other, all tangled together with hundreds of vines until it became this thirty foot high ball of branches with red and orange leaves. There was absolutely no way to get through it, and it was so dense that there was no point in trying.

"What the hell?" Darion said, horror-struck.

"Don't panic," Dad said calmly. "Just trust me, and do as I do."

He reached out with his hand and wrapped his fingers around one of the vines. Demetri exchanged a puzzled glance with Darion, but they both turned and copied him.

The vines started to slither like snakes, making Demetri jump in his skin. They slid up and out of the way, bending back branches along with them--Before long, a brilliant red and orange tunnel stretched out before them.

Demetri wasn't entirely sure what he was looking at. He couldn't help but notice its beauty, but he was becoming more confused by the second.

"Follow me," Dad said simply as he swaggered confidently through this magically appearing tunnel, and Demetri beamed brightly as he followed suit with Darion tip-toeing nervously behind him.

"What is all of this, Dad?" Demetri asked cheerfully.

"You'll see..."

And see they did. After a short stroll through the tunnel, they found themselves in their favorite clearing, surrounded by the tangled mass on all sides, but just as beautiful and peaceful as they had left it. Relief swept through Demetri's heart upon seeing the meadow--but it was nothing compared to what he felt when he looked toward the tree house--

--The fort that they left was barely a frame, yet here it stood high in their tree, completely finished. Gaping upward with his jaw wide open, Demetri could make out two perfectly circular floors made of gorgeous petrified-white wood. Brimming with delight, he looked over at his brother and beamed a smile as broad as his dropped jaw would allow.

"UNREAL!" They both shouted as they ran forward to check out their own special place--but they couldn't find a way up. Still in euphoric shock, they ran back to Dad to ask for help.

"How do we get up?" Demetri asked breathlessly.

"How did you *do* this?" Darion interjected, clearly gob-smacked.

"This wasn't me," Dad replied, shrugging his shoulders.

"--Then *who?*" Demetri asked impatiently.

"Let's just say that Gema called in a few favors," he said mysteriously through his loving grin. "The wall is a special gift from some green light friends of hers. The vines and bushes have been trained to sense your blood, and they will only open a path for someone in the Anbidian family."

"*Seriously?!*" Demetri squeaked, bursting with excitement.

"So cool..." Darion said, clearly taken aback. "...and the hideout?"

Demetri didn't think it was possible at the time, but Dad's smile spread even wider.

"Let's just say that *I* called in a few favors," he winked. "Happy Birthday boys. There's a rope ladder hidden in a tunnel around the trunk of the tree--just as you requested, Darion."

Darion beamed with joy and sprinted for the tree, and Demetri sprinted right behind him. In that moment, he realized exactly what Dad and Gema had done for him and his brother. They may not have been going off on some wild adventure, but they had a place to start one--a special hidden home for their great adventures... After all, in this newly discovered world of grace and beauty, of danger and excitement--they had no idea what amazing journeys the rest of their lives had in store for them--and they couldn't wait to find out.

40364494R00212

Made in the USA
Lexington, KY
02 April 2015